Also by Debra Moffitt

Only Girls Allowed
Best Kept Secret

The Forever Crush

THE PINK LOCKER SOCIETY

Debra Moffitt

ST. MARTIN'S GRIFFIN

NEW YORK

THE FOREVER CRUSH. Copyright © 2011 by Debra Moffitt. All rights reserved. Printed in the United States of America. For information, address St. Martin's Press, 175 Fifth Avenue, New York, N.Y. 10010.

www.stmartins.com

Library of Congress Cataloging-in-Publication Data

Moffitt, Debra.
 The forever crush / Debra Moffitt.—1st ed.
  p. cm.
 Summary: Eighth-grader Jemma has a crush on Forrest, so when he asks her to be his fake-girlfriend because he wants a break from real relationships, she agrees, thinking that it will give her a chance to make him like her.
 ISBN 978-0-312-64504-5
 [1. Dating (Social customs)—Fiction. 2. Secret societies—Fiction. 3. Peer pressure—Fiction. 4. Middle schools—Fiction. 5. Schools—Fiction.] I. Title.
  PZ7.M7245Fo 2011
  [Fic]—dc22

                                                        2011000017

First Edition: May 2011

Printed in April 2011 in the United States of America by RR Donnelley, Harrisonburg, Virginia

10 9 8 7 6 5 4 3 2 1

The Forever Crush

One

For the first time in my life, I opened Facebook and changed my profile to say "in a relationship." Then I went one step further and identified the boy I was in a relationship with: Forrest McCann. Joy bubbled up from a deep, unknown well inside my chest. It burst into a towering fountain when I went to Forrest's page and saw he had done the same.

Tiny speck of a problem, though: Forrest is my almost-real boyfriend, my forever crush.

Oh, he's not pretend, like an imaginary friend. He's a real boy. But we've made a pact to pretend we are going out with each other. Or rather, he offered me this part and I took it. Forrest said he was worn out with girl trouble and wanted to be officially out of the dating scene for a while. Here was his plan: If I was his pretend girlfriend, no one would bother him. It would be like being on base when you're playing tag. No one can touch you.

There was no chance I'd say no. I wanted to get closer to him and this seemed like one rung on that very long ladder. We already knew each other well, if not recently well. I've known Forrest since preschool because our parents are friends. But something changed along the way, at least for me, and I started to crush on him in an overwhelming way. Forrest is all grown up now and he absolutely fascinates me.

The trouble is Forrest fascinates lots of girls. There was Taylor and then Piper (briefly), and now the Bouchard sisters, Lauren and Charlotte, and—it seems—every great-looking girl in a 100-mile radius. Why? He plays football and sings in a band and his beachy brown hair falls over his left eye. Enough said?

I know what you are thinking. *Jemma, duck! Get out of the way! Big mistake being made! Do not be someone's pretend girlfriend!*

Oh, how I wish you were there at the time to give me that good advice. But I was on my own when I accepted Forrest's unusual proposal. I swore that I'd tell no one the truth about us. Why did I agree to this? Well, I guess it's because Forrest had just told me something true about himself: He was having trouble with girl-boy relationships and wanted a break. It made me extraordinarily happy to help him solve this problem. When it comes to tall, broad-shouldered, green-eyed Forrest, I rarely use anything like logic or reasoning to guide my decisions. I rely instead on my crooked heart, which was about to send me on a meandering journey.

Looking back, being his pretend girlfriend was a lot like being in a foreign country, where I didn't speak the language or understand the customs. But like all journeys of my heart, this one would start and end with Forrest McCann.

Two

"Love is in the air!" Kate sang out to me when she found me in the girls' restroom. In her hand, she held the invitation to Ms. Russo and Mr. Ford's New Year's Eve wedding, but I knew she meant love was in the air for me and Forrest, too.

"Are you so totally, over-the-moon, can't-sleep-a-wink happy?" my best friend asked. She wore a look of such happy hopefulness that it almost made me weep.

"Sure, yes. Of course. I'm happy. It's great," I said.

"Details, details, I need to know all the details," Kate said. "Wait! Don't say anything yet. You can tell me and Piper at lunch."

And before I could gather my thoughts enough to respond, Kate had spun around and was heading out the door. But in almost the same second she stepped out of the restroom, she poked her head back in and said, "And now you will have the perfect date for the wedding. Aahhh!"

Her over-the-top, excited "Aahhh!" echoed in the restroom after she left. Thank God, I was alone. No one was there to see me lean on the restroom sink, for support, and look at myself in the mirror. Who was I and how long could I keep this up?

I wished I could turn to the Pink Locker Society instead of being one of three people in charge of it. This is totally the kind of question the PLS could help someone with. But since it was my problem and I was stuck inside of it, I had zero creative ideas about what to do. I couldn't just submit a question to the PLS Web site and wait for an answer. Or could I?

Three

F AT or NOT?

That was the screaming title inside a spiral note-book that was making its way around the eighth grade. The rules were simple. Everyone's name was listed next to columns labeled "FAT" or "NOT FAT." People put stars in the boxes to "vote" for which one they thought you were.

I've always been thin and I don't even need to shop in women's clothing stores yet, but still I raced to my name. Phew, a long parade of stars under "not fat." Then I started poking around looking for other people's names. Piper, not fat, of course. Bet, not fat. Forrest, not fat.

Gorgeous teen model, Clem Caritas, definitely skinny, skinny, skinny. Clem's little sister, I had noticed, was now a sixth-grader. Mimi looked nothing like the stunning Clem. She was not overweight, but Mimi was shorter and rounder than her willowy big sis. It was enough to make me glad I had no brothers or sisters—no one to compare myself to.

I continued to scan the list until my eyes stopped and stared at Kate's name. Instead of all her stars being bunched in the "not fat" column, it was mixed. An almost even number of people put their stars under "fat" and "not fat."

"Ugh, no way," I said to myself. Unfortunately, this was math class and Mr. Ford heard me.

He shot me a look.

I nodded and remembered that I could not get caught with this notebook. It was secret from teachers, who'd almost certainly punish me for having it, let alone writing in it. We were supposed to be working on homework, so I figured I could enter my votes now and it would look like I was working on parallelograms and rhombuses (or is it rhombi?).

I inked a big blue star under "not fat" for Kate and went on through the rest of the list. I was kind, I think, and only listed as "fat" people who really did seem overweight. Like Emma Shrewsberry and Alex Donovan. Kate was, well, just Kate. "She's got an hourglass figure," my mother had said. Kate was bigger than me but not in a bad way. I hoped that Emma, Alex, and especially Kate did not see this notebook. When I was done, I tucked it into my purple English folder and went back to work on my geometry.

I wondered how Forrest had voted in the Fat or Not book. Had he given me one of my "not fat" stars? I figured that was what was expected of a boyfriend, that he would stick up for me in this kind of situation. It was another way of saying I was good-looking or at least not bad-looking. I glanced over my shoulder to the back corner of the room to see if maybe he was using a distinctive pen. Then I could have scanned the book again and figured out if he had already rated me.

But then I saw that his writing instrument of choice was just a boring old yellow number two pencil. I spun back around quickly because I didn't want him to catch me looking at him. He wasn't my real boyfriend and it took all my strength to remember that.

Four

Once you understand the cafeteria, you can be super efficient. And just about every eighth-grader knows the routine. You can pack your lunch, bring your own drink, and maximize the time you and your friends have to gab it up before it's time for afternoon classes. Or, you can buy your lunch, but you have to get there lickety split or you'll be at the end of the line. By the time you pay for your lunch, you will have hardly any time to eat it.

I used neither of those tactics today. I packed my lunch but left my raspberry seltzer water in my locker on purpose so that I could spend time in the lunch line getting a drink. I then moved at a snail-like pace to the cafeteria and stood in line instead of just jumping to the front to grab my milk. By the time I reached our table, Kate was halfway finished with her PB&J and Piper was pushing around the remnants of her spinach salad.

"Where were you, Mrs. McCann? With Mr. McCann?" Piper teased.

My stomach did a somersault and my face reddened.

"She's blushing," Kate said with a grin.

"Stop it, you guys. I was getting a drink," I said.

"Okay, we'll buy that if you tell us the whole story. Start at the beginning. He came over to your house for dinner and . . . ," Kate said.

"Right, my parents invited his whole family."

I took a moment to set out my lunch components: grilled chicken wrap, apple, milk.

"And?" Kate said.

"Yes, and?" Piper said.

"My mom thought they were moving and I guessed they almost moved, but they're not moving," I said.

"Okay, we know that," Piper said. "Remember? My mom was their realtor, so I know they're not moving. Go on, please."

"You're not mad at all, Piper?" I said.

Piper had gone to the eighth-grade dance with Forrest and I had been so upset about it. But she moved on.

"He and I were together for, like, half a minute," Piper said. "I'm glad you finally upgraded your crush to a boyfriend." She leaned over to give me a side hug.

Upgraded to a boyfriend? Not exactly.

I started eating my lunch, thinking this would pause the inquiry. For a while Piper and Kate just watched me eat. Bite after bite, all was quiet and they watched me, like I was an egg they were hoping would hatch.

"What?" I said, my mouth finally clear of food.

"Maybe you are new to this, but having a boyfriend is, like, the funnest thing ever to talk about," Piper said. "In fact, I think talking about boys might *actually* be more fun that being with them. So, umm, what's your deal?"

"Yes, Jem. We're dying here for some details. What happened Saturday night at your house?" Kate said.

"Yes, and why wouldn't you have called us—or at least texted—like, immediately?" Piper asked.

I took a deep breath and began. I told them how we were stuck with Trevor most of the night, but that Forrest told me that he was having trouble with girls.

"He said, 'Girls want answers and I don't have any answers, Jem.'"

"Awww. He called you Jem," Kate said. "Did he kiss you then, outside by the grill?"

"No," I said. "He squeezed my hand."

"He held your hand?" Kate asked.

I shook my head no. Then I told them what happened the next morning, when I ran by his house and saw him shooting baskets.

"I asked him to run with me and we ran all the way to Price's Dairy and back. He was really hurting near the end," I said.

"So is it then that he asked you to go out?" Kate asked.

Technically, no. After our run, he asked me to be his pretend girlfriend.

I nodded yes. "We drank ice water together on his back porch until his parents got up to go to church," I said.

Forrest had said, "I don't want to mess anything up for you. So if you're, like, going out with someone now, or there's someone you like, forget about it."

"And he said he liked me and we had a lot in common and why didn't we go out. Seize the day and all that," I said.

"Forrest said 'seize the day'? That so totally doesn't sound like him," Piper said.

"He said something like that, anyway," I said.

"You don't remember his exact words?" Kate said. "I thought you wrote down everything he ever said to you in that diary under your bed."

I do. The real truth is all there.

"Kate! TMI, don't you think? I mean, I have a boyfriend now, so I can't be all blabby about everything," I said.

"*I* am," Piper said.

"She is," Kate agreed.

It was right then that I was about to say something

witty about how Piper had a lot more to tell, with her having a different boyfriend every week. But in a flash, Forrest walked right up to our table, punched me softly on the shoulder, and said, "Hey," before heading to history.

Five

At study hall, we slipped into the stairwell and descended into the basement, which was our dismal new PLS "office." I wanted to get to work on the Pink Locker Society Web site, but Kate and Piper tried to shake some more Forrest details out of me. I would have liked to ask them what they thought about his soft punch to my shoulder. What did it mean? But they thought he was my boyfriend and that's a pretty normal boyfriend thing to do. I guess I didn't expect him to actually touch me during this fake relationship of ours.

I resisted saying anything more and my friends let it go, partly because we had so much work to do. With literally hundreds of questions coming in to the Pink Locker Society, we were trying to answer at least one question a day. But seven a week was hard, especially because the questions girls sent in weren't always easy. Sure, there were the standard ones about when—oh, when—will I get my period? But there were also ones like this:

Dear PLS,

I'm just an ordinary girl and I know I'm not skinny, but I didn't think I was fat. That was until I saw my ratings in the Fat or Not book. Twenty-two people said I was not fat, but eighteen people said I was. I asked my mom and she says I'm not, but she's my MOM. What's she going to tell me—the terrible truth? I want to know how to know for sure if I'm fat and how to get thinner, if I am. And FAST. I would like to know exactly who those eighteen people were who said I was fat. So mean!

Confused Girl

"I feel so bad for her. Confused Girl is probably Emma Shrewsberry," I said.

"My money is on her, too," Piper said.

"What should we tell her?" Kate asked.

Usually, we take a few moments to think and then we start talking at once, brimming with ideas of how to answer a girl's question. But in this case, it was just quiet and quiet and more quiet.

"I guess I can ask the nurse, right? She'll know something about it," I said.

"Um, she'll know something, but she won't know what to say to make her feel better," Kate said.

"Well, all we can do is try," Piper said. "Jemma, Kate—who wants this one?"

"I'm not qualified to answer," Kate said, stone-faced.

"What is that supposed to mean?" I asked her.

"I'm on the fat list, as you both probably know."

Piper and I both looked at Kate with pity. I knew Piper had seen the book and had already filled in her votes.

"Okay, whatever, I honestly don't care at all. It's dumb," Kate said. "But I'm worried for other people."

That was so like Kate, always thinking about others before herself.

"I'll look into it and give Emma a really nice answer," I said. "I'll be supportive, not mean. I promise."

"Please tell me you guys didn't vote in that terrible notebook," Kate said, eyeing both of us.

Piper bit her bottom lip but didn't say a word.

"I have the notebook in my backpack," I admitted with embarrassment.

"You have it? You filled it in?" Kate asked, looking hurt.

I told her that Tyler Lima had given it to me and that I was supposed to pass it on to Charlotte Bouchard. Charlotte and her twin sister, Lauren, were slim as could be. They also both completely, obviously liked Forrest. I wonder how they felt now that I was dating him. Well, now that it appeared that I was dating him, anyway.

Piper sighed dramatically and shook her head at the laptop screen.

"Really?" she said, as if talking directly to the computer.

"What's the matter?" I said.

Piper spun the laptop around and showed us the next message in our queue:

Attention PLS,

I think you are gross and discusting and you talk about gross and discusting things. If you don't shut yourselves down, I'll shut you down myself.

Your worst enemy

"That's unfriendly," said Kate.

By my count, this was the seventh threat we'd received in the last three weeks. It started with this one:

I know who you all are. Stop now or you'll be sorry. Very sorry.

From there, they seemed to repeat a theme—that what we were saying on the PLS was foul, sick, or otherwise "inappropriate." The use of the "I" word frightened me because that's the word Principal F. used to describe the Pink Locker Society after he forced us to shut it down. And before we restarted it on our own. Shhhh!

"One threat, fine. Two threats, still no big deal. But we're talking about SEVEN threats now," I said. "It's time to do something."

"Like what?" Kate asked.

Six

You are a link in the pink chain.

I n between threats, and our daily barrage of questions from girls, the PLS had been getting a new category of messages. These were less disturbing (hurray!), but still unusual. They all began, "You are a link in the pink chain."

We assumed they were sent by someone older because they always included some kind of historical factoid related to the PLS or girls in general. I guessed that the messages were from Ms. Russo, or her anonymous source—the former Pink Locker Lady who a while back sent me the Kathrine Switzer race number. She was the first woman to run in the Boston Marathon. Since I'm on the track team now, I had pinned that to my bulletin board at home for good luck.

Sometimes, I wondered if Edith was writing the notes. She had invited us to be in the Pink Locker Society at the start of school, but we hadn't heard from her since we were shut down. I wasn't sure she'd approve of how we had restarted the PLS on our own. (Though I would have loved to get back in touch with her if it meant we could get back into the swank office she had set up for us behind the pink locker doors. Our new basement office was dingy and gross.)

These pink chain messages reminded us that we were not the first Pink Locker Society members—and we wouldn't be the last. Nor were we the first group of girls to try to do good stuff. I imagined myself, Piper, and Kate as a chain of pink daisies, rather than a thick metal chain that clanked, like in a haunted house. It was clear from the messages that our flowery chain reached way back in time.

You are a link in the pink chain. With pride, we point to 1832, when Maria Weston founded the Boston Female Anti-Slavery Society in Massachusetts. With help from freedom-loving women—and men—slavery was outlawed in the United States in 1865.

Honestly, I didn't know what to make of the pink chain messages.

You are a link in the pink chain. In 1869, Susan B. Anthony, Elizabeth Cady Stanton, and Lucy Stone formed two groups that pushed hard to give women the right to vote in the United States. It took more than 50 years. The 19th amendment was ratified in 1920.

Was someone hoping that we would do something world-changing? Right then I was content just to help the girls who wrote in with basic questions about middle-school life. And I just assumed everyone thought girls and boys were equal. I was much more interested in talking about how all girls were not equal, but they should be.

For instance, certain girls at my school, like Taylor Mayweather and Clem Caritas (and sometimes even Piper), seemed to think they were better than everyone else, probably because they were so pretty and grown-up-looking. They were the girls that boys wanted. I was an eighth-grader who still didn't have her period. And my boyfriend wasn't really my boyfriend.

Oh, I know pretty, popular girls have problems, too. Even the most gorgeous girls with seemingly perfect lives are worrying about something, trust me. The Pink Locker Society had hundreds of questions from girls to prove it. And I guess, being a link in the pink chain, it was our job to help them, too.

But my mind today was focused on my own distressing dilemma: Could I just keep being Forrest's faux girlfriend forever? Would I one day be his fake fiancée, his pretend wife? I tried to tell myself that this was my best chance with him, even if it was just make-believe. But I also had to admit that this was not a problem Piper, or Clem, or Taylor—or even Kate—would ever have. It felt like I was the only girl in the universe who would *ever* have this problem.

Telling Kate and Piper the truth would have been embarrassing, and then the truth would be out there, like a hamster out of its cage. Piper would say something too loud and everyone would find out. Or Kate, in her sweet Kate way, would accidentally reveal the awful truth. This potentially embarrassing moment would be far worse than the time I got caught on video crawling out of my locker (I had been inside our gorgeous secret office for a Pink Locker Society meeting). And it would be worse than people thinking—as they briefly did—that I had a crush on Trevor McCann, Forrest's brother, a sixth-grader.

So I had to do something, right? I did what hundreds of girls had already done. I texted a question to the Pink Locker Society.

Dear PLS,

Love your site! I hope you can help me with this one. My crush asked me to be his "pretend girlfriend." I said yes because it seemed like a really good way to get to know him better and convince him to like me for real. Is this a good or a bad idea? And if it's a bad idea, how do I tell my friends the truth? Do I have to fake-break up with my fake boyfriend?

In Love (for real) With a Pretend Boyfriend

I looked down at my fingers on the phone's keyboard. Would I really send this in? I spotted an eyelash on the back of my hand. For good luck, I blew it away and hit send.

Seven

Being someone's pretend girlfriend drained me daily. There was no drama between us, like I'd seen with other eighth-grade couples. But I was being an actress all the time, living a secret life. We had so much more contact with each other now that I almost missed the days when he was just my crush. At least then, if he was nice to me, or said hi, I knew it was real. But when your pretend boyfriend sits near you at lunch or smiles at you, what does it mean? I had no idea. It just wasn't real. Or if part of it was real I'd never be able to figure out which part.

I needed lots more time to think because my feelings were changing each day. So there I was: head leaned back in the car, eyes closed, letting Mom drive me home from track practice, when she blurted it right out.

"Jemma, I hear you and Forrest are an item," my mother said.

She made it worse by reaching over and giving me a playful swat on the knee.

I had no idea she knew. And if she knew, who else knew? Dad? Mrs. McCann? It was like someone dropped a heavy jar of marbles and they scattered everywhere. I didn't know where to begin.

In my panic, I couldn't speak so I just wrinkled my nose and shook my head, still facing the windshield. It was like she presented me with a plate of chilled creamed spinach. No, no, take it away! My wish was that the conversation would end immediately and the topic never be raised again.

"Are you saying no? Or are you saying you just don't want to discuss it?" Mom asked, smiling now.

"I'm not saying anything," I said, and scrunched down in my seat.

"Well, I just wanted you to know that I knew and that if you ever need to talk about anything, I'm here. First love can be confusing," Mom said.

OMG, now she was talking about love. I wonder if I would survive if I flung myself out the car door right now. Probably not.

"The feelings can be quite intense. I was young once, you know," she said.

"Okay, Okay, I get it. Next subject, please," I said.

I reached over to turn on the radio and cranked up the volume to a conversation-stopping level. I pretended to be engrossed in the song, which I didn't even like. I knew only the chorus for sing-along purposes. When the refrain was over, I looked for something, anything, to occupy my mind and my hands as I sat trapped and imprisoned in the front seat next to my mother.

I fiddled with the glove compartment, looking for nothing in particular. It was then that I heard the sound of my mom starting to cry.

"Mom? Mom? Are you all right?" I asked. "Did somebody die?"

Between her sobs, she told me that no one had died and that she was just a little sad that I seemed angry with her. And that it "just hit her" that I was growing up so fast. But as for why she was crying while driving through our neighborhood, she said could not explain it.

"I haven't a clue what's come over me," she said.

Then she laughed and wiped her tears with the back of her hand. I laughed with her, but I didn't like seeing her acting not normal. As far as her crying history, Mom cried like grown-up people do. She cried at funerals and at sad movies. And sometimes when they played those patriotic songs on the Fourth of July. But she was not a weep-at-the-drop-of-a-hat mom.

I was so lonely in my own thoughts about Forrest that,

for a moment, I wished that Mom would have some instant knowledge of the whole situation. Then maybe she'd tell me what to do. Sometimes I got so lonely I told our cat, Donald Hall, about the whole thing. He wasn't a frisky, friendly cat, but I think he understood. More than Mom, at least. Within minutes of the Forrest revelation, she was chatting to me about everyday boring stuff, like what time I needed to wake up the next morning and how I should *please, please, please* stop using a new towel every time I took a shower.

"Really, Jem. Seven towels a week. Who are you? The Queen of England?"

Eight

A better friend would have just tossed the Fat or Not notebook into the nearest trash can and put an end to it. But instead, I handed it to Forrest when we were at our lockers. They were side by side, which gave me plenty of opportunities during the day to make eye contact, say something witty, or appear so irresistible that he would be overcome with emotion and ask me to be his REAL girlfriend. But these encounters were rarely satisfying. Typically, he said nothing at all. Or just hey.

I decided to give him the Fat or Not notebook because I thought it might make for a good topic of conversation— something that could have sparked more than just a hey. His back was turned so I watched him getting his books from his locker. I didn't want to get caught staring or startle him. I tried to look busy in my locker, but when he stood up I made my move.

"Forrest," I said, "have you had this yet?"

"Had what?" Forrest asked.

"The"—I whispered—"Fat or Not book."

"Oh, that. No."

"Do you want it?"

"Um, no. Yes. I mean, I don't know."

"Either you do or you don't. Which?"

"I don't know. I don't want to get in trouble or have people be mad at me."

"So I should keep it or you want it?"

Really, he was exhausting me.

He took the notebook and leaned back on his now-closed locker. He lifted one knee and pressed the bottom of his foot against the locker door, striking a pose while he flipped through. I wondered in that moment if he was trying to look cool for me. But then, instead of meeting my gaze, he looked over my left shoulder.

"McCann! McCann!" squealed Charlotte Bouchard as she came winging by. She casually rested her elbow on Forrest's shoulder and looked into his eyes.

"I do believe you have something of mine," she said, grabbing the notebook. "Gotta go, but keep in touch."

We both watched her run down the hall.

"I guess that's that," I said.

Just as I was about to search my brain for a new topic, Bet arrived.

"Hello to you both. Did I just see you with the Fat or Not notebook?"

"You did, but Charlotte took it," I said.

"Shoot," Bet said. "I'm working on a broadcast about it and I just can't seem to get my hands on it."

Bet was always working on a broadcast. She's the anchorperson for Margaret Simon Middle School's only TV show, *You Bet!* It isn't exactly real TV. Bet produces her video reports and the principal broadcasts them on the school's TV network every Friday afternoon.

"If I see it again, I'll grab it for you," I said.

"Thank you, Jemma. You're the best."

Bet squeezed my arm gently, in a conspiratorial way, and left. Bet knew how much I liked Forrest and for how long. That squeeze was her way of congratulating me. I looked at Forrest to see if he caught this girl-to-girl signal.

"Jemma," Forrest said, "I have to ask you something."

I swallowed and waited.

Please God, don't let him break up with me already.

So many girls liked him, and it seemed like it would be just a matter of time until he'd like one of them in a real way. And then I'd just be a failed experiment for him, something he might joke with me about at our high school graduation.

"There's this movie thing that I'm invited to this weekend, the day after Thanksgiving. People are bringing girlfriends, so it would be weird if you didn't come."

"Oh."

"Unless you have something else to do. I guess I could say you have to go visit your grandmother or something."

"My grandmother lives in Florida. It takes, like, eighteen hours to drive there."

"So you want to go to this thing?"

"Um, sure. Why not? Might as well keep up the act, right?" I said this to check if this was him asking me out on a real date, or a date to keep up appearances for our pretend relationship.

"Yeah. I think everyone is convinced," Forrest said.

Nine

I waited, like lots of other girls, for the Pink Locker Society to answer my question. We were getting so many messages from girls wanting help that I had to pull my question from the very deep inbox and ask that we take it on.

"What about this one who says she's got a pretend boyfriend?" I asked Piper and Kate during a PLS meeting.

"Yeah, I saw that one," Piper said. "But do you think it's even real? Who has a pretend boyfriend?"

It took all my strength not to answer, "It's me! It's me! And it's driving me crazy."

Kate swooped in, so naturally helpful.

"I think it could be true. And she says she really likes our Web site. Why not?" she said.

"Okay, Jemma. That falls into the topic of embarrassing things, so I think it's yours."

"Why is that so embarrassing?" I asked Piper, hoping it wouldn't blow my cover.

"An imaginary boyfriend? It's like she's going around introducing everyone to her invisible friend Harvey, a six-foot-tall bunny rabbit," Piper said.

I stayed quiet and let Kate defend me.

"Well, if you look again at the message, it's not that she invented a boyfriend out of thin air," Kate said. "She and this real guy are pretending to go out. Seems different than a completely invented boyfriend. I'll take this one."

Hurray! I was going to get Kate's four-star advice without her knowing that it was me.

"Speaking of boyfriends," Piper said. "Jemma, I hear you're going to dinner and a movie with Forrest on Friday night."

"Dinner and a movie" turned out to be something dreamed up by the beautiful Clem Caritas. Yes, my not-so-friendly locker neighbor. Once a month, a select group of eighth-graders made dinner at someone's house and then went to see a movie. I had never been invited before.

"Oh, goodie," Kate said. "Me and Brett are going, too."

"And I'll be there with Dylan," Piper said.

Dylan was the latest of Piper's boyfriends. He was in ninth grade—a high-school guy!—and played ice hockey.

"A triple date . . . ," I said a little blandly.

I was worried about all those eyes on Forrest and me. Surely these girls who knew me so well would be able to tell that Forrest and I were a big fat fake.

"Moving on," Kate said, turning back to the laptop. "Oh crud, study hall is almost over."

It was hard to keep track of the time down in the school basement. There were no clocks. Were we really still the Pink Locker Society if we hadn't stepped through our pink lockers in weeks? I tried not to think about our beautiful and well-appointed offices now that they were off-limits. It felt like forever ago that we opened our lockers on the first day of school and saw them—the pink locker doors inside our regular lockers. Ever since Principal F. shut us down, we had to keep jackets hung up in our lockers to hide the secret pink doors.

But while I was dreaming of our comfy couch, ergonomic desk chairs, and conference table, Kate was still thinking about Emma Shrewsberry and that question about being fat. It was assigned to me and I hadn't come up with an answer yet.

"What have you found out?" Kate asked.

"I'm working on it," I said.

This was like saying "I'm almost there," when I actually hadn't even left the house. I assumed there would be some kind of easy answer to her question. There wasn't.

"Well, remember that it's a two-part question," Kate

said. "She wants to know how to find out for sure if she's fat or not. And, if she is, she wants to know how to lose weight fast."

I made a mental note to talk with Bet, who was already investigating the Fat or Not notebook.

"Ugh," Piper said.

"What?" asked Kate.

"It's nothing. Just a stupid message," Piper said.

"Let me see," I said, and turned the laptop toward me.

> *The girls who write this stuff are trashy and cheap. What if boys see this? STOP now!!*
>
> *Your worst enemy*

The three of us were silent for a moment. When girls called girls stuff like that, we knew it was code for other more shocking words. They were like curse words, but it was more than that. They were words that hurt girls and made them feel deeply bad about themselves. Parents would fall over with shock if they knew how often girls in middle school hear them.

A mean eighth-grader, now moved on to high school, thankfully, once called me one of those shocking words on the school bus. I was only in sixth grade and I didn't know what it meant. I had to ask my mother, which led, as you might expect, to my mom actually boarding the bus the next day to discuss the matter with the bus driver.

Once I knew the definition I felt better because it in no way applied to me. I hadn't even kissed a boy then.

"There is this high-school girl," Piper said in a small voice. "She hates me because I'm going out with Dylan. I think it could be her."

Piper had been called those mean names before, plenty of times, actually. You could tell by her quiet voice and the way she stared at the floor as she spoke. Piper sometimes joked, "Beauty is my curse." But this was one of those times that it actually seemed true. More often than us regular girls, the prettiest girls got called trashy, cheap, and worse.

"I'm sorry she's being mean to you, Piper," I said. "But that would mean she knows that you specifically are in the Pink Locker Society. Very few people know, right? High-school girls probably don't know about us."

"I guess that's right," she said.

"Then who is it?" Kate said. "Who else would be so angry about periods, bras, and boys?"

"Yeah," I said. "And if this person hates us so much, why don't they just stop coming to our site?"

Ten

On Friday morning, when I told my mom about dinner and a movie, she teared up again. It wasn't a full-scale sob, like in the car, but there were tears in her eyes. This time my dad was there.

"Oh babycakes, why don't you go lie down a while?" he said, smiling.

Do all parents use pet names for one another? There's "honey" and "sweetheart," which are fine, I guess. But my parents tended to these random, cutesy names. Mom called Dad "Dearheart," "Honeybun," and "Pookie." Dad, for his part, called her "Mary Bell" and "Babe." I had previously expressed my desire that my parents stick to calling one another by their actual names, Mary Beth and Jim, but they had ignored my requests. They also continued to call me "Cupcake" even though I told them this was not a nickname suitable for a thirteen-year-old. Of course, I hadn't minded being called "Buzzy." But that was only because Forrest gave me the nickname after the whole beehive incident.

"Why is she acting so weird?" I asked Dad in a whisper after Mom left the room.

"Oh, she's just . . . just a little worn out," he said.

I didn't like the idea of my mother being worn out. I liked Mom to be, well, Mom—certainly not one to cry about me going out to the movies.

"Am I allowed to go?" I asked Dad.

"Go where?" he asked.

Dad was not usually my point of contact for getting permission to go here or there. It was awkward as I explained the group date aspect.

"You're dating now? Oh, I don't know, Jem."

"It's not a date-date. It's a bunch of people. I'm not five anymore, Dad," I said, a little louder than I intended.

"No, I suppose not," he said. "But let's check with your mom."

When I went to Mom and Dad's room, she wasn't there. I could see her bathroom door was closed, so I broke a rule and started talking to her through the door. She *hated* this. I gave her the essential details and waited for her reply. What I heard sounded a lot like Mom throwing up. Had she eaten too much turkey and pie the day before?

Eleven

Sometimes the most awkward thing in eighth-grade life is not being able to drive. We all felt grown-up and we were going to a grown-up event: dinner and a movie. But we would be arriving at Clem's house in the backseats of our parents' cars. They would stop in the driveway, or (please no) get out of the car and say hello to Clem's parents.

It was decided that Mrs. McCann would take me and Forrest and also pick up Kate and Brett. Piper, lucky duck, was getting a ride from Dylan's older brother who had his driver's license. Clem was already there since it was her house. I didn't know about the other girls—Clem's friends—who I hardly knew.

Clem's house, conveniently, was in a neighborhood close enough that we could walk to the movie theater.

My parents—I could hardly stand the thought—would be picking up the four of us after the movie.

I felt so nervous that I wished I could run to Clem's house instead of getting driven there by Forrest's mom. I got ready way too early and then I changed clothes once, twice, three times. I broke into a sweat and wondered if I smelled. Should I shower again? There wasn't time, so I just added more deodorant and wiped my forehead with two squares of toilet paper. I sat on the edge of my bed and felt like I might throw up. This wave of nausea reminded me of Mom earlier today and further rattled me because I still did not understand what was going on with her. She didn't seem sick, even after the barfing.

Knock-knock-knock.

I flew out of my room, but I could hear Dad already at the door. I froze and listened. I heard the door open and then voices—mostly my dad's.

"It's just that, Forrest, Jemma is my little girl and I would hate for her to get hurt," Dad said.

OMG.

"Uh, sure," Forrest said, "I understand. We're friends, mostly."

Mostly?

"You're a good kid, I know that," Dad said.

My choices were stay put and let this torture continue or bound into the living room and become part of it.

When I made it to the living room, I saw Forrest standing in our foyer. The autumn sunset was at his back. He looked happy to be rescued.

"You remember what I told you, Forrest," Dad said, and clapped him on the back.

I shot my dad a look that said, "Enough!"

We went out the door and started walking toward the McCanns' green Jeep.

"We'll be there to pick you up at ten forty-five!" Dad called.

I waved and settled into the backseat. I wished Kate and Brett were there, but they were our next stop.

"Hi there, Jemma," Mrs. McCann said, eyeing me in her rearview mirror. Her voice was a little more singsongy than normal. Everyone was acting differently now that Forrest and I were "going out." I wanted to ask Forrest what my dad had said, but not in front of Mrs. McCann. So I just sat there in the quiet, grateful when Mrs. McCann put on some music.

When we stopped for Kate and Brett, they jumped in the backseat with me, and Forrest moved up front with his mom. That was a relief because with three in the backseat, I was nervous I would be squished next to Forrest.

Clem's house was white painted brick and had a purple door. Inside, it was like a cozy country cottage. This surprised me because Clem is an actual teen model with a portfolio and I always pictured her living in a fancy-pants city apartment. But seeing as though we were in the same school district, it shouldn't have surprised me that her house was just two neighborhoods over and no more cosmopolitan than mine. She hugged all the guests hello at the door, which was really surprising. The girl who hugged me was the same girl who said little more than a cool hello to me at school, even though our lockers were side by side.

Clem and her mom had dinner nearly cooked. The warm spicy scent wafted throughout the house, from the cozy kitchen to the cozier living room, complete with fireplace and sweet brown dog sleeping on the hearth.

"I hope everyone likes pad thai," Clem said as she breezed through carrying appetizers on a silver tray.

I love pad thai, so I breathed a sigh of relief. I will eat most things, but if Clem was serving something gross, like stew, I would seriously have had to bail on dinner.

"What's pad thai?" Forrest asked me.

"It's sooooo good. Noodles in a sweet-sour-salty kind of sauce. And bean sprouts and peanuts."

"Oh man. I can't eat that," Forrest said.

"Are you allergic?" I said.

"No, I just don't eat that kind of food. I thought she'd have pizza or something," he said. "Last time, she had hamburgers and ribs."

Note to Forrest: *Please don't mention the time you were here with your old girlfriend.*

"Well, you could just try a bite," I said. "Take a little. Push it around the plate."

"But I'm starving," he said.

"I guess you can just get a snack at the movies," I said.

"Okay, I guess," he said.

"Dinner bell!" Clem sang out from the dining room.

Forrest grabbed my arm.

"Jem, you have to sit next to me. I have a plan."

Seated around the dinner table, I really felt like a grown-up. I nodded politely across the table to Taylor, even though I didn't mean it. Before dinner, Clem's little sister, Mimi, had poked her head into the living room. She was wearing a ballerina tutu and I asked if she took ballet.

"Uh-huh," she said softly.

Mimi Caritas had a sweet face, not much personal style, and always looked nervous standing in the school lobby before the first bell. Mimi was such a sixth-grader. I could tell she was trying to look cool, but she wasn't exactly sure how. Could only two years separate the tall, fabulous Clem from her shorter, baby-faced sister?

Mimi twirled her way down the hall, closer to where I was standing. But her twirl went off kilter and she spun herself into the wall. A heavy picture frame crashed onto the wood floor. When Clem heard the crash, she yelled, "No little kids allowed!" and Mimi raced back to her room.

Clem and her equally gorgeous model boyfriend, Beau, also a ninth-grader, had lit candles around the dining room. They were on the table and also behind us on tables and shelves that held heavy pottery and old glass milk bottles.

At the oval table, Kate was on my left and Forrest was on my right. Kate squeezed my knee under the blue-checked tablecloth and winked at me.

"Stop it!" I said to her in a whisper.

Worse yet, Piper kept playing footsie with me under the table. I gave her a glare as the food started being passed around. Forrest took a little of the soup and a surprisingly large portion of the pad thai.

Good for you, Forrest, trying something new.

Then I realized what Piper was up to: she was not trying to play footsie with me, she was trying to knock my foot into Forrest's foot under the table! Like a chain reaction, Piper shoved my foot and my foot knocked into Forrest's skateboard sneaker.

"Piper!" I blurted across the table.

"What? What?" she said, turning her laughing face toward Dylan.

"Sorry," I said to Forrest.

"Does everyone love the pad thai?" Clem asked. She was drinking water with lemon from a wide-mouth wine glass. She held the glass as if she was at a glamorous Hollywood party, pinky out.

"It's amazing," I said, wondering if the two of us would now be friends. But Clem didn't look at me.

"It's great," Forrest said. "Could I have some more water?"

"Sure," Clem said, getting up.

When she was out of the room, Forrest grabbed my nearly finished plate and switched it with his full plate. I laughed but before I could protest, Clem was leaning in to fill his wine glass with water.

"Thanks," Forrest said.

Clem saw Forrest's plate, which appeared to be my plate.

"Jemma, don't you like it? Eat up!" she said.

Twelve

Standing against the glass concession stand at the movie theater, my stomach felt stuffed tight with pad thai noodles. I had not imagined indigestion playing such a role on my first date with Forrest. I had plenty of appetizers plus my huge plate of pad thai. Then I had eaten most of Forrest's dinner, too.

"Water, I just need a water," I told Forrest.

"No popcorn?" he said before ordering a mega-bucket with melted butter.

"Nothing for me, thanks," Kate told Brett before joining me in the ladies' room.

I started to feel a little less sick following our bathroom stop. We couldn't find enough seats together for everyone, but we found a section of the theater where we could be close, if not side by side. The couples naturally paired off and found seats together. Forrest tugged on the sleeve of my sweater and motioned toward two seats a few rows back, on the end.

"It's better back here," he said.

We were close enough to wave at our friends, but not so close that they could hear Forrest and me talking.

"Have you been on a movie date before?"

"I've been to the movies," I said.

"On a date?" Forrest asked.

"Yeah, I think that last time I went to a movie it was October fourteenth. That's a date," I said.

"You know what I mean."

"But this isn't a date-date, right?"

"Right, but people think it is. I'm just saying that it's normal to, like, look like boyfriend and girlfriend here," he said.

"What are you saying?"

"People hold hands and stuff."

"But it's dark. No one will see us," I said.

"They'll turn around and check."

And at that moment, Piper turned around and gave me a little wave. Not three seconds later, Kate did the same thing. Even Clem seemed to be checking on Forrest and me. Clem, until tonight, had seemed unaware that I existed.

"What am I supposed to do?"

"Nothing. I'm just saying if we don't seem like we're, you know, together, they'll think it's weird. Or that we're breaking up."

"How can we break up when we're not even together?"

He laughed and reached his arm across my back and rested his fingertips on my shoulder. The next time Piper and Kate turned around to check on us, Forrest's arm was in this strange new place. They smiled and turned back around, satisfied.

The movie roared with action and a story that kept everyone guessing until the end. But I was more interested in the drama unfolding between Forrest and me. At first, he held his arm ever-so-gently across my back, like he was trying not to bother me. But as the movie wore on, he relaxed, I guess, and his arm felt heavier. Centimeter by centimeter, I relaxed in his direction, making the arm-around-me thing feel more natural. I savored the feeling, knowing I would be rewinding this moment in my head over and over again.

Since my friends checked up on me, I took a moment to see what the other couples were doing in the movie darkness. From what I could see, Kate and Brett were holding hands. Beau had his arm around Clem and they were sharing a soda. Piper and Dylan were a couple rows ahead on the left, sitting as close as they could, despite the cup holder between them. They were just black silhouettes, shadow puppets almost, against the movie screen. I kept one eye on them, I'm embarrassed to say, because I wondered if they would kiss. I felt even more embarrassed when they did. I tried to make myself look away, but I couldn't.

It was so romantic. Dylan was so into Piper. You could just tell. At dinner, he laughed at all her jokes and helped her put on her coat. At the concession stand, he bought her gummy bears, unprompted, because he knew she liked them.

"You're the sweetest thing," Piper had said to him.

Even as I enjoyed the sweet touch of Forrest's arm across my back, I knew we were different from every other couple in that theater. After the movie ended and the lights went up, Forrest extricated himself from me. He smiled at me sleepily and set the empty popcorn bucket on the sticky floor. The window for anything more to happen between us had closed for the night. Next, we were in the lobby and then outside in the cold night air waiting for my dad to pick us up.

Thirteen

KATE: Did he kiss you?
PIPER: Smooch ☺ or no smooch ☹?

Those were the texts waiting for me as soon as I flopped down on my bed and tried to make sense of the whirlwind night I'd just had. I almost texted no, but that would have led to follow-up questions. *What happened? Why not? Are you guys fighting?*

I lacked the strength to respond so I plugged my phone in its charger and turned on the shower. I did my best thinking in two places: the shower and while I was running. In the shower, I'd get so lost in thought that my parents often had to bang on the door to snap me awake.

The soothing drum of the water always helped me to think things through.

Tonight, between the shampoo and body wash, I tallied up the evening's pluses and minuses.

Pluses
Forrest and I talked and laughed.
I helped him with his pad thai issue.
He put his arm around me.

Minuses
He didn't kiss me.
He doesn't look at me in that "Wow, I'm so into you" way.
This relationship is still faker than Clem's blond highlights.

I already knew the moment that I would dwell on, examine, and re-examine over the coming days. It was fifteen or so minutes into the movie. Forrest's arm was already positioned around me, but then there was a moment when it morphed from a stiff awkwardness to relaxed coziness. He let the weight of his arm rest on me. And millimeter by millimeter, I stopped being so tense and fit myself naturally into the shelter of his arm. It was a moment I had definitely been waiting for. But it was not hard evidence. Maybe he just needed to relax his arm after holding it there for so long. And then I thought, why wouldn't he just move his arm if he was uncomfortable? And then there was that whole issue of him telling my dad that we were "friends *mostly*."

These are questions I could have asked Forrest (maybe) if we were a real couple, or that I could have pondered with Kate and Piper. They loved giving advice about guys. But how could I talk about any of this? If I were really with Forrest, none of it would be an issue.

I started hoping and praying Kate would answer my anonymous PLS question—and quickly. For good karma, I promised to start right away on my answer about the Fat or Not notebook. I had already made Emma Shrewsberry wait long enough. I started ticking off advice points in my head and wished I had a notebook with me in the shower to jot some of them down. But just as I got to thinking, Mom was knocking loudly on the door.

"Jemma, for the love of Pete, we're going to run out of water if you don't get out of the shower already!"

Fourteen

I arranged to meet Bet at Lucky's Coffee Shop early the next morning. I arrived first and ordered myself a raspberry zinger tea with double lemon. Bet knew nothing about last night and I hadn't discussed Forrest with her since this new development: me being his sorta girlfriend.

It was a relief to know that she wouldn't press me for details I didn't want to discuss. I continued to ignore my cell phone and the texts about whether Forrest kissed me or not. I would later tell Kate and Piper that my phone was out of charge (another lie—but who's counting?).

I pulled out my notebook and tried to think of all the advice I could give someone like Emma Shrewsberry about a weight problem. I sat there with the pen poised for several minutes. But what did I know about being over-weight? I was a round and chubby baby, but as I got older, I turned thin, like my dad. In fact, I had wished at times that I would gain weight, but my doctor said I was "healthy and consistent on the curve"—whatever that meant.

I guess I could suggest that Emma talk to her doctor, but this seemed like bad advice because once you're an older kid, you only go to the doctor, like, once a year. Maybe she could text her doctor. Do doctors answer texts? It would be helpful if they did.

Bet slid into the booth with a steaming cup of some-thing that smelled like gingerbread. Christmas was on the way.

"I heard you went to dinner and a movie with Forrest last night," Bet said with a knowing smile.

I sighed and said yes.

"Can we talk about that later?" I asked. "I want to see if you can help me with a PLS question."

Bet looked a little hurt, but she pulled out her own notebook and pen and said okay.

"Since you're interested in this Fat or Not list, I thought you would be able to help," I said.

Bet sighed and nodded.

"A girl has written in—we think it's Emma Shrewsberry—to ask how she can find out if she's actually fat," I said. "She also wants to know how to lose weight quickly."

"Well, I don't know all that much, but I do know that she shouldn't try to lose weight fast," Bet said. "It's possible she doesn't even need to lose weight."

I remembered looking through the pages of the Fat or Not notebook. Kate had received some votes in the fat column, but with Emma, it was a landslide win for fat over not fat.

Bet looked grim as she swirled a packet of sugar into her cinnamon spice tea.

"I wasn't going to say anything, but I actually do have some research on this. And I might as well give it to you because I don't need it," Bet said.

"Why not?"

"Principal F. says I can't do a report about the Fat or Not notebook. He says it's not appropriate, and that I should do my next report on good hand-washing techniques in advance of flu season." Bet rolled her eyes.

Bet's weekly show on our school's TV channel, MSTV, had started out really well. She won a contest, beating out both Taylor Mayweather and Clem Caritas, for the opportunity to have her own show. But almost immediately, she ran into problems with Principal Finklestein.

He refused to let her broadcast part two of her investigation into the history of the Pink Locker Society. Only a few of us knew what she learned—that in the 1970s the PLS office was ransacked and their printing equipment stolen after they supported something controversial at the time: girls' sports! I didn't have the heart to tell Bet that now there were more newsworthy angles to pursue, like how we were getting scary threats and all about the pink chain messages.

Bet had done a few of her *You Bet!* shows with no problems. She reported on recycling and on how to avoid choking on food (I was the star of that one). But for a second time Principal F. was telling Bet not to broadcast her report—to replace interesting stuff that people would have wanted to watch with hand-washing instructions.

"It's censorship, plain and simple," Bet said. "I'd like to sue but my parents said I should try to work 'within the system.'"

"So you can't do anything about the Fat or Not list?"

"No, I can't report about 'any subject that may reflect negatively upon Margaret Simon Middle School.'"

"That stinks, Bet," I said, "but if you tell me what you know about being overweight, at least I can help Emma, or whoever it is. It's got to be Emma, don't you think?"

"Probably, but then there are all those girls who think they are fat and aren't fat at all."

"I hadn't thought of that," I said. Sitting there with Bet made me remember why I liked her even though she wasn't one of my besties. She had a mind that worked hard and she had ideas that were not the obvious ones. I had been not-so-secretly happy when she dropped out of the PLS to do her shows. But we kinda-sorta actually needed her.

Bet shook her head like she was trying to shake the memory of Principal Finklestein from her head. Then she laid out what she knew.

"If someone wants to know if they're overweight or not, they can use the body mass index."

"How do you use it? What does it do?"

"I'm not completely sure. When I Googled it, you get an equation of sorts. It's a math problem."

"So I'll have to ask Mr. Ford, not the school nurse?"

"Maybe both of them?" Bet said. "That's what I was going to do. Back when I had a show, that is."

"You'll have a show, Bet," I said. "You're not the kind to give up."

Fifteen

For the most part, we didn't want grown-ups involved in the Pink Locker Society. We liked calling all the shots. None of us had told our parents that the PLS was back up and running, and we prayed daily that Principal Finklestein wouldn't find out either. But the one adult we were grateful to have in the know was Ms. Russo. She was our confidante and unofficial adult adviser.

I wanted to tell someone quite desperately about the threatening messages. It was kind of like we were being bullied and I wanted that person to STOP. I mean, do you want to hear that some mystery person lurking around your school thinks you're trashy or that someone is out to get you? We certainly didn't. So it felt good when we caught

Ms. Russo one day after school and told her what was going on. We had shared the first of these messages with her weeks ago, but we hadn't told her that they'd continued—and that they had gotten even meaner.

"And you don't have any clue who might be sending these?" she said, elbows resting on her desk.

It was filled from edge to edge with papers, pens, markers, handmade treasures, and at least three coffee cups from today, yesterday, who knew? There was a lot to look at on her desk, but these days my eyes always settled on her left hand and that beautiful new engagement ring.

We told her that we had no clue, except that we thought it was a strange coincidence that Principal F. had often used that disturbing term *inappropriate*.

"Oh, come on, girls—it's not him. Trust me, if he wanted you to shut down he'd go straight to your parents again," she said.

Piper, Kate, and I slumped low in our chairs, almost in unison. Just thinking about Principal Finklestein going to our parents made us shudder.

"I don't like the idea that someone is threatening you so personally," Ms. Russo said.

And we hadn't even shown her the really cruel message. You know the one.

She said she'd call upon her Pink Lady contact, the one who had been feeding her information for awhile. This former Pink Locker Lady—years ago that's what they called themselves—apparently worked at the school but didn't want to be identified.

"It's good to have someone on the inside," Ms. Russo said, "who will share information with me."

Ms. Russo started riffling through layers of papers and artwork on her desk. And then, like she had been fishing with a line, she pulled out a narrow rectangle of paper. She handed it to me, so I was first to see that it was a home-made bookmark that said "STOP the PLS. It's gross and discusting!"

"The person can't even spell *disgusting*," I said, shocked. "Where did this come from?"

"Someone's been putting them in library books," Ms. Russo said. "We have a friend in there and she's trying to get rid of them, but it's difficult. There are two thousand books in our library."

So the librarian was on our side, too. I'd seen Ms. Russo and Mrs. Kelbrock having lunch together.

"Let me see that," Piper said, grabbing the flimsy book-mark from me. "We are not disgusting. This is ridiculous!" Piper exclaimed when she read what it said.

"Well, some people *are* grossed out about periods and stuff," Kate said.

"Yeah, but you get over it—and it doesn't make us disgusting," Piper said.

Ms. Russo said we should be looking at the bookmark for clues. It was written on a strip of looseleaf notebook paper—the same kind of paper everyone at school used. The handwriting didn't look familiar. But the person was a bad speller, so maybe it was a sixth-grader?

"Even if we did know who, what would we do? Complain to the principal?" I asked.

"No, I guess you couldn't do that and stay anonymous and in business," Ms. Russo said. "But please keep me apprised of these threats and what they say."

"Could it be a grown-up?" I asked, scared at the thought.

"We don't know. I guess the person could be trying to look like a kid, with the chicken-scratch writing and the misspellings," Ms. Russo said.

"So is Mrs. Kelbrock the former Pink Locker Lady who you've been talking to?" I asked.

"Aren't you a probing thinker, Jemma? No, it's not her. My contact is older and she wants to stay anonymous," Ms. Russo said.

Ms. Russo added that she would ask her about the threats and for any help she might provide on that.

"I say we just keep doing what we're doing and ignore it all," Piper said.

Easy for Piper to say.

"Don't be intimidated, that's the spirit!" Ms. Russo said, in her best "positive teacher" tone.

Piper was ready to change the subject, having plucked a wedding magazine from the edge of Ms. Russo's desk.

"Let's talk wedding!" Piper said.

Ms. Russo smiled and seemed happy to shift gears.

"Well, we *are* in a dilemma right now over the cake. White chocolate mousse or raspberry filling?"

"Both," we all agreed.

Sixteen

I decided to think hard about who could be the myste-rious bookmark-maker. It could be someone like Taylor Mayweather. She was always causing a stir and had once before hacked into the PLS site. (She was caught, but went unpunished.) But Taylor would never have fashioned such a crude bookmark. She would have used sparkles and ostrich feathers, not plain old paper and blue ink.

A boy could have done this. I mean, a boy probably wouldn't care about the prettiness of his bookmark. And I know boys can be grossed out by girl stuff, like peri-ods. I had seen that in sixth grade when they split us up for "the talk" about puberty and stuff. Some boys annoyed us girls by saying gross stuff afterward. But what boy would be so bothered by a girls-only Web site?

It could be someone thousands of miles away. This was the Internet, after all. There was nothing stopping someone in Australia from visiting www.pinklockersociety .org, but this argument fell apart at the bookmarks. How would this devious Aussie get bookmarks into our school library? It seemed like a huge stretch.

We all went to the library at least once a week with our classes, but no one would have enough time to work an operation like this during class.

But wait a minute. If you were in Library Club, you'd have plenty of opportunity.

Eureka! Library club members were in the library every day at study hall, and they were often doing stuff like shelving books.

I had been a library club member in sixth grade. It's a little nerdy, I know, and I am almost embarrassed by how much I enjoyed the solitary task. At first, I thought: How can this be a club when you can only whisper to the other club members? But then I came to enjoy the quiet, orderly activity. You followed the alphabet or the Dewey Decimal System and put things where they belonged. Simple and calming, kind of like running is for me now. I secretly wanted to return to the library club as a member, but I was worried people would make fun of me.

So back to our suspects: the entire library club. I needed to get the members' names and eliminate them one by one.

I texted Kate and Piper without thinking, so proud of my detective work and possible lead. Kate texted back immediately.

KATE: Where u been?
ME: Phone dead
KATE: Lib club? Shazam!
KATE: How's Forrest? Good night?
ME: Yep. GTG

Piper wasn't far behind with the text response. She utterly ignored my library club insight.

PIPER: Answer the smoochie ?
ME: Privacy, pls!
PIPER: THAT MEANS HE KISSED YOU!

No, Piper. It doesn't.
My cell phone sprang to life in my hand. It was Piper, calling.

"Okay," she said. "You need to spill it."

"Um, no I don't," I said.

"You're no fun."

"What did you think about the library club? It could be someone who's in it."

"Sure," Piper said sarcastically. "Let's bring them all in for a lineup."

"You're not taking this seriously."

"You're taking this too seriously, Jem."

"Well, it is serious. Someone's threatening us. Saying we're, you know, bad influences or something."

"I always try to let that stuff roll off my back. Hey, I called because I heard something and just wanted you to know."

"What?"

"Some girls were talking at cheerleading and they were being mean about you and Forrest. It was Taylor, Clem, and that group."

"What did they say?"

"They were just like, 'I don't know why he's with her and blah blah blah,'" Piper said.

Yeah, me either. Oh, wait, he's actually NOT.

"I don't want to upset you, Jem. I just wanted to let you know. I was like, 'Duh, Clem, they were just both at your house for dinner and a movie.' He obviously likes you, Jem," Piper said in a happy voice.

"Obviously. Right," I said.

I ended the call and the whole thing hit me in waves.

First wave: I thought Clem might have actually been my friend now, so it hurt to have her talking behind my back.

True, she paid me no attention before the other night. But I thought it might be different since then.

Second wave: I was horrified that people were picking me apart—and more importantly, picking apart my "relationship." It was like I was a criminal and they were sniffing me out, saying to themselves: This just doesn't quite add up. Forrest and Jemma do not make sense. He is too good for her.

Third wave: If these girls are saying mean stuff about me, they are probably saying it right to Forrest's face—after all, they barely talked to me until I started going out with Forrest. I worried he'd break up with me. Why? Because he wouldn't want to be seen going out with someone who was, let's face it, not nearly as beautiful and popular as his recent girlfriends.

I wished I could take some kind of medicine or potion that would make me grow up faster *right away*. I was still shorter and less grown-up-looking than all of my friends. Was there a magic product like, say, Boobtastic, that could make my molehills grow into mountains? I could see the infomercial for that. Anytime I complained about this to Kate or Piper, they'd say I was "cute." Why did that always sound like second prize?

Personal progress was happening, but it was achingly slow. I had gone up a bra size or two. And I had some signs, *if you know what I mean*, that my period would arrive sooner rather than later. These were good signs that I was, indeed, growing into an actual woman. But I wished it would all happen overnight and I would wake up looking like the grown-up, ready-to-conquer-the-world me. Then maybe Forrest would keep me as his pretend girlfriend and, eventually, want me as his real one.

Seventeen

*W*elcome to my bewildering, pink world. Here are the first three PLS messages Kate, Piper, and I opened today in our dark, dusty school basement headquarters.

Message 1:

> *Dear PLS, I heard that if you whisper the Pledge of Allegiance every night before bed for 28 days, then on the 29th day, you'll get your period. Is that true?*
>
> *Signed, A Late Bloomer Who Loves Her Country*

Message 2:

You are a link in the pink chain. Have you ever run for class president? If so, then you might want to thank Jeanette Rankin. In 1916, she was the first woman EVER to win a seat in the U.S. Congress. After serving, she dedicated her life to promoting peace all over the world. Remember, you are a link in the pink chain!

Message 3:

I've asked nicely but time is running out. END THE PLS NOW! This stuff just shouldn't be up here. It's privit. From Your Worst Enemy

So there it is, we have a classic period question (Answer is No! BTW), we have an encouraging pink chain message (Go, Jeanette!), and another lovely anonymous threat with its telltale mispelling. Contrary to the message, the threat-sender did *not* ask nicely before. She called us "trashy," but whatever. I was getting fed up. Can you tell?

"Maybe whoever is writing these pink chain messages could ease up on the history lessons and help us get rid of this stalker," I told Piper and Kate.

"Oh Jem, that person's not stalking us. It really could be just prank stuff," Kate said.

Piper asked what I was so scared of. Maybe she was

right and it was just some jokester in library club. She had a point, but I did, too.

"It's no joke that this person is leaving anti-PLS bookmarks in the library," I said.

"True," Kate said.

"Okay," Piper said. "Let's ask Russo to get us some backup here—and to see about getting back our old office."

"Like that will happen," I said.

"Well, as my mom says about selling houses, 'If you want something, you gotta ask,'" Piper said.

Piper pushed us back toward our regular business. While we had answered a bunch of easy questions in the last week (bra-size issues, leg-shaving dilemmas), neither Kate nor I had answered our more complicated questions. That is, I hadn't answered the weight question and Kate hadn't answered my pretend boyfriend question.

"I'm ready to go on that one," Kate said. "I'm going to tell her to come clean to her friends and to break up with the guy."

I held my breath.

"What if she doesn't want to?" Piper asked. "What if she likes being in a fantasy world, pretending that she's this guy's real girlfriend?"

"Right," Kate said. "It could be hard for her. But you can't live a fake life with a fake boyfriend and mislead your friends."

I cleared my throat. They both looked at me, waiting

for me to say something. But I just smiled meekly and looked back at my notebook, where I pretended to write something down.

"Onward then," said Piper. "Jemma, what have you got on the Fat or Not thing?"

I gave them my recap, saying that I now understood what BMI was. I talked with Bet and I asked both the school nurse and Mr. Ford.

"It's complicated, but basically BMI is a number that tells whether you're underweight, at a good weight, or overweight. You put your height and weight in a formula and it gives you your number. You can do it online," I said.

"That's good," Kate said. "We can just put the link in there so she can do it herself."

"But I'm worried that if she does that it will just spit out a number that says 'You're fat,'" I said.

Kate winced a little, like she had just taken a punch. I needed to remind myself that this was a touchy subject for Kate, too.

"You're kind of plotting yourself on an X-Y axis, like in geometry," I said. "Your weight, over time, are like points on the graph. If you connect the dots, they make a curve. That's why my doctor says I'm 'consistent on the curve'— I've always been thin and though I gain weight I'm still in the same percentile," I said.

"You're losing me," Kate said. "What did the nurse say?"

"She said you can get your BMI number, but you need a doctor or nurse to really make sense of it all," I said.

"And what about the losing-weight-fast part of her question?" Kate asked.

"Well, there's no simple answer there either," I said. "People younger than eighteen shouldn't really diet. You know, like, eat only grapefruit or something crazy like that. At least that's what the nurse said."

"So what's she supposed to do if she comes up fat in that formula?" Kate asked pointedly.

"I don't know, but the nurse did give me four tips," I said.

I pulled out my notebook page, where I had them in a bullet list. I held it up for them to see.

- Eat more fruits and vegetables
- Drink water instead of soda and sugary drinks
- Get an hour of exercise every day
- Understand that it's normal for a girl's body to change during puberty. Hips get wider and figures get curvy.

"No offense, Jemma, but what's the difference between fat and curvy?" Kate asked.

I had no answer. I wondered if there would ever be anything curvy about my body. Kate continued. "Eat right. Get exercise. Everyone says that and it's not very easy to do," she said.

"I'm sorry, Kate, if you can do better on this one, then go ahead."

I was actually a little angry at Kate for how she answered my question about Forrest. That's probably why I was so snippy.

"Come on, you two never argue. What's up?" Piper said.

I was miffed at Piper, too, come to think of it.

No, Piper. I'm not living in a fantasy world by fake-dating Forrest. It's more than that to me.

Neither of us answered Piper's question.

"Jemma, I think your answer is good," Piper said. "Kate, we can't spend our whole year on one question."

"I-I'm sorry," Kate said. "I got carried away, I guess."

"I did the best I could, Kate," I said. "That's all I ever do, you know that."

I was worried I might cry, right there in the school basement, and admit everything to them both. But Piper put an arm around each of us and pulled us into a group hug.

"C'mon girlies, hug it out," she said.

And we did.

Eighteen

*W*e needed Bet, I decided. With her video camera and her inquisitive mind, I knew she'd have some good ideas for how to locate and stop our stalker.

That's right. I said stalker.

Again, I met Bet at Lucky's. We rode our bikes there, as usual, but the December weather was turning colder. It wasn't so bad when you were walking, but the wind whipped my face as I pedaled uphill into downtown. Well, it was "downtown" in our small town—a few restaurants, a hardware store, a drug store, a fancy dress boutique, and a place that made homemade ice cream in summer and boarded its front in winter.

Bet and I arrived within minutes of each other, hung our jackets on hooks, and settled into our back booth, red-cheeked. Mugs of cinnamon tea steamed below our noses.

"The bookmark bandit—I love it!" Bet said. She pulled out her notebook and settled into note-taking position.

"I don't love it," I said.

I told her about my hunch about library club members and about the succession of threats, including how whoever it was called us "cheap and trashy."

"Ugh. What does that even mean when you are in middle school? None of you guys are cheap or trashy," Bet said.

"Well, thanks. I guess that's a compliment," I said.

"I mean it's not trashy to tell girls about basic stuff that will happen or already has happened to them," Bet said.

"Uh-huh," I agreed.

"And this person is worried about boys seeing it? I really doubt boys are visiting the Pink Locker Society. I mean can you imagine Forrest surfing around on that girlie site? And even if he did, who cares?"

She was getting fired up now. This happened with Bet a lot. I laughed in a nervous way. Just the mention of Forrest's name could set me off.

"Forrest spends most of his time on his fantasy football Web site," I said.

"Exactly," Bet said.

I liked that Forrest had named his fantasy football

team Six Strings after the six strings on the guitar he played. He was a guy who was a jock and played sports but was also an artist—someone who might sing me a song someday.

Oh, it was so tempting to just spill it all to Bet. She was a good listener and she would keep my secret. And she always wanted to hear both sides. I thought she might see some other way than the route Kate advised. I didn't want to break up with Forrest and admit the lie to everyone.

"So the trick will be to get the names of all the library club members. And some surveillance would be nice," Bet said.

Bet thought the instigator of all this was clearly angry—why else go off and attack us personally? She also guessed it was probably a girl. I told her that Ms. Russo was friends with Mrs. Kelbrock, the librarian.

"Excellent—a great lead," Bet said. Then she took a last sip of her tea and stared into the empty cup.

"Oh, Bet. I'm so sorry. I've been talking on and on about the Pink Locker Society and all our problems, and I haven't even once asked about your show."

I had noticed that *You Bet!* had not been shown for the last few weeks. She did the hand washing show as requested but that was it. On the announcements, Principal F. said the show was going on a temporary hiatus and would be back with a "new format that I'm very pleased about."

Bet said her report on the Fat or Not list was already prepared and ready to air, but Principal Finklestein said no. She said she had interviewed a bunch of people on the list, including Emma Shrewsberry.

"By the way, Emma said she did not write in about the Fat or Not list."

I didn't blame Emma for denying it.

"And Kate?"

"I asked to interview her, but she didn't want to talk about the notebook, not even off the record. I told her I didn't think she was fat at all," Bet said.

"So you'll never be able to show that report?" I asked.

"Principal F. wants me to make my show more lively and fill it with 'good news,'" Bet said. She put up finger quotes around the words.

"That could be . . . okay, right? You'd still have a show," I said, trying to be encouraging.

"I guess, but I'd rather report on things people actually care about. Do you really want to know more about Hangnail Awareness Week?"

"You made that up," I said.

"Maybe so, but you get the idea. You're lucky, Jemma. The Pink Locker Society can just do whatever you guys want," Bet said.

She was absolutely right and—lightbulb!—a fabulous idea was born.

Nineteen

Kate and I don't fight. Well . . . at least not much. We had that testy moment about the weight and BMI thing, and we've had other spats. But in general, we get along well and we keep the drama to a minimum. That's mostly because of Kate, I think. She's just so easygoing and not at all competitive. I depend on her yoga voice and generally chill attitude about life. Not so on this particular day. She texted me:

KATE: Why is there a VIDEO on OUR Web site?

That was my fabulous idea. Our Web site, www.pink lockersociety.org, could host Bet's show on the Fat or Not list. In fact, I thought the PLS site could host her show permanently. I mean, who needed Margaret Simon TV when you had the whole Internet? So I just went ahead and posted it up there. I thought Kate and Piper would be impressed with my creative decision-making skills and my technical ability to make the video work on the PLS site.

The report was brilliant, I thought. Classic Bet. She had really gone in-depth and interviewed tons of people—students, teachers, our school nurse, and a doctor. She explained body mass index. She gave all sides—kids who wrote in the book said they just did it for fun and didn't really think anything much about it. The people who were called out as fat—even people who got only one star in the fat column—were pretty upset.

Emma Shrewsberry was so brave to be interviewed.

"I know I'm overweight and I'm working on it," she told Bet. "I'm going to the doctor and I've lost twelve pounds. I don't like being made fun of, so I didn't appreciate that list," she said.

I wondered if my tips (eat more fruits and veggies, etc.) had helped her.

"What I would say to anyone who knows they're overweight is that they need to find real friends. Maybe you'll lose weight and be healthy. But you'll never get there without friends who like you right now, as you are," Emma said.

Bet then interviewed Emma's two best friends. They were not overweight, but they said they now exercised as a trio and tried to do simple stuff for Emma, like eat healthier foods when they had sleepovers together.

It was such an upbeat story, it was hard to understand why Principal F. didn't want to air the piece. I received an immediate congratulatory text from Piper. So it surprised me to receive the exact opposite response from Kate.

KATE: Thanks a lot, Jemma. YOU ARE NOT A GOOD FRIEND!

I immediately called Kate's number.

"Kate, what is going on? Why are you so upset?"

"Aren't we the Pink Locker Society, as in we're all part of the group and we should make important decisions together?"

"Yes, but I thought you would like that I put Bet's video up there. You were the one always encouraging me to be friends with her."

"Be friends with her all you like, but did you see her show?"

"Yes, I saw it."

"Stop it, Jemma. You know exactly what I mean."

"No, Kate, I really, seriously do not."

"When Bet showed the pages of the Fat or Not list, in the notebook, my name was there. It was *first* on the page. How do you think that makes me feel?"

"Kate, I didn't even see it."

"It's not bad enough that everyone in the eighth grade saw the notebook. Now anyone who has a computer will know I was in that book as a fat chick."

I remembered the shots of the notebook. They went by so quickly, I didn't see anything.

I heard Kate sigh loudly. And she was sniffing some, too. I worried that she was crying.

"Can you get her to take it off?" Kate asked, her voice quieter now.

"Well, she'll be really disappointed because she was just kicked off MSTV. And this seemed like a place where she could put her *You Bet!* shows without any hassles," I said.

"Jemma, you just do not get it."

"Tell me," I said.

"I used to look in the mirror and see myself—not perfect but a normal-looking girl. Now, every time I see myself I see my worst parts."

"Kate, you're beautiful. Everyone says so."

"Yes, but eighteen people also said I'm fat."

"Who cares?" I said. "People aren't really thinking when they fill that list out. It's just a stupid thing, for fun."

"It's not fun for me," Kate said. "I did that BMI thing and my number was too high."

"Don't be mad at me, Kate, please."

"Then help me."

I asked her, "What would you do, if you were in my position? Whatever it is, that's what I should do."

Twenty

ow I really felt like a bad friend. Not only had I
been lying, for weeks now, to Kate about me and
Forrest, but I just accidentally humiliated her in front
of the entire Internet. I needed to fix it, but how could
I do it without devastating Bet? She was so happy when
I said I'd post her videos on www.pinklockersociety.
org. She hugged me and said I was the nicest person
she'd met since coming to Margaret Simon Middle
School. But how was that possible when Kate saw it all
so differently?

Luckily, Kate never held grudges. She was still my
friend and she didn't send me any more mean texts. But
she did bring up Bet's video more than once and asked
when it would come down. Kate knew it would not be

hard for me to remove it. She could have done it herself even, but she was waiting for me to do the right thing.

I couldn't bend the truth like I might with, say, my mother. My mom was technologically stuck in 1985. She still has one of the original Walkman cassette players. She also has a cell phone without texting capabilities and says she's fine with that.

But it was not fine with me—especially on Thursday when I never got her phone calls telling me she'd be late picking me up from running club. I usually don't put my ringer on, because I mostly text and I don't want it going off in school. But all Mom does is call the regular way. I didn't hear her calls and I sat there after school, wondering where she was.

She wanted me to try to get a ride home from someone else. But I didn't notice the messages until too late. Running club had long ended. It was already dark and everyone had left except for Mrs. Percy in the office. I was out in front of the school and I could see her puttering around in the glass-enclosed front office even though it was after five thirty. Then a few minutes later, with Mom still not there, I saw the lights turn out and figured she'd be coming out soon. I secretly hoped that she'd exit through some side door.

Mrs. Percy had a reputation. Ms. Russo told me, "She doesn't suffer fools gladly." She was blunt and direct and did not seem to edit her thoughts much. I heard the scrape-scrape of the heavy front school doors and knew she'd stop and say something to me.

"Jemma Colwin, what in heaven's name are you still doing here?"

"My mom's coming. She'll be here soon."

"Would you like to go inside and call her?"

Another low-tech woman, Mrs. Percy was. At home, she probably still had a phone that was hooked to the wall with a twisty cord.

"No. Thanks. I have my cell phone. She called me earlier. Now she's not answering," I said.

I was thinking I'd just add this to the list of weird behavior Mom was exhibiting lately. I hoped she was OK.

"Well, I'll just wait here with you until your mother comes," Mrs. Percy said. "Can't have you all alone out here."

She sat down with a *harrumph* on the wooden bench next to me, my backpack the only buffer between us. This was even worse than talking to Forrest. I had no conversation ideas for me and the crabby school secretary. I had hardly ever thought of her except to hope and pray that she'd be on vacation if I ever got my period at school. When the school nurse was off at a district conference or working a half-day at another school, Mrs. Percy filled in. I had once heard a boy in my class tell her he had a headache.

"Me, too," she had said, without looking up from the high counter where she stood. "Now, go back to class."

I couldn't imagine a safe topic for the two of us so I stayed quiet on the bench.

"You run track?" she asked.

"Yeah. I just started this year." I looked down at the patch of pavement between my two sneakered feet. My running shoes were neon orange so cars would see me. (Mom's idea.)

"Do you know there was a time when we had no girls' track team whatsoever?"

"Uh-huh."

"Back in the day, there was a girls' basketball team, but they didn't travel or have uniforms."

I turned my head to face her and nodded. Why was she telling me this? And more importantly, I knew I had heard this before. Was it in a pink chain e-mail?

"There was cheerleading, but it was that 'rah-rah-sis-boom-bah' kind of cheerleading. Not throw yourself up thirty feet in the air and dance like a hootchie-cootchie girl cheerleading."

I laughed at "hootchie-cootchie." She seriously sounded like my grandma. And then it hit me.

"You're Patricia," I said quietly, almost to myself.

"Who, me?" she said, and smiled. Then she winked at me.

"Patricia" wasn't her real first name. It was Adele and

86

people called her Addie. Patricia was the fake name Bet gave her when she interviewed her on camera about the original Pink Locker Society. Bet had shown her only as a silhouette behind a curtain and even computer-synthesized her voice so that no one would know who she was. At the time, I thought I recognized that rat-a-tat way of speaking, even with the scrambled voice.

"I'm actually glad you know," she said. "You're doing a nice job with the Pink Locker Society."

"Thanks," I said.

It was so weird to be taking a compliment for this, especially from her. She had told Bet all about the PLS getting shut down in the 1970s. It was after they had openly supported some female athletes at Yale who protested so they'd have locker rooms like the guys.

"I want to help you with this bookmark problem you have," Mrs. Percy said.

She said she knew about the "Stop the PLS" bookmarks and how they continued to be slipped into books. Whoever it was had slipped them into books by Meg Cabot, Judy Blume, Laurie Halse Anderson, and even *The Daring Book for Girls*.

"Janet—I mean Mrs. Kelbrock—has been on the lookout, but she hasn't caught the person yet. She thinks it's happening after school."

"I think it's someone in library club, probably a sixth-grader," I said.

"Could be. I hope we can rule out grown-ups, but people of all ages can be cruel," she said.

Was she referring to Principal F.?

"You must be the person Ms. Russo has been talking to," I said.

"You got it," she said.

"You sent me the Kathrine Switzer race number. You were in the old PLS."

"You're putting it all together now," she said. "Do you want to try your mom again?"

I did and got her.

"Mom? Where are you?"

"I'll be there in three minutes. I really wish you'd pick up your phone once in a while," she said.

"Where were you?" I asked.

"A doctor's appointment. See you soon."

Now I was worried. I wanted to know and I didn't want to know why Mom was at the doctor. She'd been weepy and tired and now needed to go see a doctor?

But Mrs. Percy wanted to tell me her plan. She said she and Mrs. Kelbrock would set up our pink laptop to monitor the security cameras in the library. They'd keep an eye on the cameras, too, and maybe we'd catch the villain.

OK, so Mrs. P. wasn't clueless in the technology department. I didn't even know there were security cameras at school.

"Good" was all I said because, at that moment, my mom appeared at the curb. She rolled down the passenger side window.

"Oh, Mrs. Percy. I'm so sorry to make you wait. It's been a crazy day." She smiled, shook her head, and her hands left the steering wheel in a flapping gesture to indicate just how crazy.

"No worries," Mrs. P. said. "Jemma and I had a nice chat."

Twenty-one

In the car, I finally blurted out what I had been think-ing about and worrying about: What was going on with Mom?

"Why are you late? Why were you at the doctor's?" I asked.

She only smiled and said she had something exciting to share, but she wouldn't reveal it until dinner. I was happy to see she looked fine and she seemed more cheerful than she had in weeks.

Dinner was quick because we just picked up a pizza. At home, Mom set the table and I made a salad. I tore the lettuce, sprinkled in the carrots, and chopped some red peppers. Then I topped the whole thing with cranberries and pecans. An artful, professional job, I must say. Except that Mom kept dipping her hand into the big salad bowl and stealing the pecans.

"I just can't get enough pecans for some reason," she said. "I've been craving them all week."

My dad laughed out loud in response and I tried to figure out why that was funny. I've been hungry for certain foods before and no one found that hilarious. Around the table, I was only a bite into my pizza when she revealed the big news.

"Jemma, we are going to have a baby. I'm pregnant."

My dad smiled at me and took Mom's hand. I stopped in mid-chew. This seemed impossible. When you're thirteen and you've been an only child for thirteen years, you kinda figure that's just how it's always going to be.

"I know. I know," she said. "I'm shocked. Your father's shocked."

Dad nodded and grinned goofily.

"But I'm so happy," she said. "You'll finally be a big sister."

"Table for four!" Dad called out, and then clinked his water glass with Mom's in celebration.

"Wow," I said, still getting used to this news.

Mom came over and hugged me. I hugged her back, but I was still absorbing it all. I used to wish for a baby brother or a sister. Did I still want one? I wasn't sure. They told me the due date was June 21, the first day of summer. I stayed through dinner and listened to my parents talk about when they'd tell my grandparents and how they'd make a baby room out of our guest bedroom.

"I say we don't find out if it's a girl or a boy," Mom said. "Let it be a surprise."

"I don't know if I can handle any more surprises," Dad said, and laughed.

I stayed through dinner, but I was also feeling the need to be alone. There was too much going on. I now had a major life change ahead of me and the following pre-existing problems:

1. I was about to upset one friend (Bet) to help another friend (Kate) by taking the video off the Pink Locker Society Web site.
2. The PLS still had a stalker. The latest message said, "Your time is running out!"
3. I had a boyfriend who was not really my boyfriend.

Our contact was minimal, but what contact I had with Forrest was usually public. He "liked" stuff on my Facebook page, stopped by our lunch table when he was done eating, and stood near me if we were out in a group somewhere. Now that our school's football season was over, there were basketball games to go to on Friday evenings. Forrest decided not to play so he could focus on his music. His band was newly formed with some different members. They now called themselves Eleven-Eleven (11:11).

I hoped they named themselves after those two special minutes of each day when I always made a wish. But I couldn't bring myself to ask because I worried this was a babyish habit of mine. Not to mention that most of my 11:11 wishes had something to do with Forrest.

At basketball games, he sometimes sat next to me on the top bleacher, high above the action on the court. One time he gave me a pin that said "Go Fly a Kite," but it's just something he got for free at a kite store. I attached it to the lapel of my blue wool coat.

Forrest didn't send me notes or say I was pretty or buy me gifts. Kate's and Piper's boyfriends—and I suspect all normal boyfriends out there—did that. I thought of how Christmas was approaching—Ms. Russo and Mr. Ford's wedding was New Year's Eve, in fact. Would Forrest buy me a gift? I wondered what the right gift would be for him. I couldn't be too thoughtful or sentimental with the present. This was all just an act.

But measuring my every action and reaction was wearing me out. Not to mention all the lying. My friends would ask how Forrest was and I'd usually say, "Great!" But I had nothing more to add. No details, no anecdotes, no "Forrest said the cutest/nicest/funniest thing the other day" stories. And with regard to kissing, I refused to answer, but let Piper and Kate assume that we had.

Yet there were moments—like the arm around me in the movies—that seemed *real*. And there were times when we talked that I made him laugh. And this one time he seemed to really listen when I was talking about this problem with the "Stop the PLS" bookmarks and how Piper, Kate (and now Bet), and I were trying to catch this person. It was a whole domino effect: If these bookmarks attracted attention from the wrong people (Principal F., for instance, or one of our parents), people would know the PLS was up and running. They'd shut us down for good and I couldn't bear the thought. I noticed that I was clenching my fists as I explained it all to him.

He asked what I'd do if I noticed the bookmark bandit on the surveillance video. I said I'd head right over and confront the person. I wasn't sure this was true, but liked thinking I'd be so brave.

"Well, be careful," Forrest said. Pretty caring, I thought.

Another time, we were the first two of our group to meet near the water fountain before school. Had we truly been dating, I imagine this time would have filled up naturally with chitchat and whatever sweetness passes between eighth-grade couples. But Forrest and I ran out of stuff to talk about. I thought about telling him about the baby, but I hadn't even told Kate yet. Forrest and I just stood there together, in awkward silence. Where else could we go?

On other days, we were saved when a third friend arrived or when the football coach stopped by. But when no one approached, we were faced with the hard reality

that the two of us didn't really have all that much in common. I thought only I minded, but Forrest broke the silence.

"Why do you care about it so much?" Forrest asked.

"It?"

"The PLS," Forrest said.

The question struck me silent at first. I had an answer,
but I was surprised at how genuinely interested he seemed.

"It's the first thing I've been in charge of," I said.

He nodded.

"And I like helping people."

He smiled slightly and I am 99% sure that he was
thinking of how I was helping him by being his fake girlfriend.

But these moments were too few and I mostly felt sad
about him. My heart always pointed me in Forrest's direction, but I started to wonder if my heart might be steering
me wrong. I would have talked it over with Kate, or even
Piper, but of course I couldn't. It was like the having an
elephant in my bedroom. Try as I might, I kept running
smack into it.

Twenty-two

All day Saturday, I cut off communications with the outside world and forced myself to work on a presentation for American History. "Did you know Betsy Ross was a real person but no one's ever proven that she sewed the first American flag?" Well, now you do. I did a whole PowerPoint on it.

Mom seemed more like herself after her doctor appointment and picking me up so late. She was still napping in the afternoons, baby-related I guessed. When I emerged from my room post–Betsy Ross, it was my dad who was emptying the dishwasher. I stood at our kitchen counter using the family calendar to count how many more weeks until Ms. Russo and Mr. Ford's wedding. Just three!

"Are we ever going to decorate for Christmas?" I asked.

"Eventually," Dad said.

I thought a New Year's Eve wedding was *beyond* romantic. I wondered if Ms. Russo would carry roses or gardenias, like my mother had carried at her wedding. Or maybe she'd just wear a fur muff since their ceremony was outside. Yes, outside. I started thinking about what I'd wear and if I could talk Mom into buying me something new—velvet, off the shoulder maybe. It was the next official date for me and Forrest.

Mr. Ford had kept the promise he made the night of the Backward Dance, when he proposed to Ms. Russo. They invited all the eighth-graders to the wedding—my first wedding invitation ever. When I saw the invite, the location of the reception confused me. To fit everyone, they were having it *outside* at a place called Gibraltar. Outside on New Year's Eve? Mom said it was an old house with gardens outside, but nothing would be in bloom in winter.

"They must be doing tents," Mom said.

I pictured the army green canvas camping tent that we used on our rustic vacations. That was not what I had in mind for my first spin as a wedding guest. I was hoping for some fancy hotel, but I guess if they did it at an expensive place, they couldn't have invited more than a hundred of us eighth-graders to join the celebration.

I was so glad I had the wedding to look forward to. That Saturday night—like most weekend nights—stretched before me like a big snooze. Being an only child has its plusses, of course, but one of the downsides is that it's just the three of you. And since Mom was having low-energy issues, I knew that it would be nightgowns and TV by nine.

A sister—or even a brother—might have livened up the evening. Though I hear that when you have them, you fight or they won't hang out with you when you want them to. I guess in six months I'll know what it's like. I had seen Kate with her brother and sister and I knew they played marathon games of Monopoly on Saturday nights. I imagined my new, bald, diaper-wearing brother or sister sitting across the table from me with a fanned-out wad of Monopoly money.

After a snack, I realized I needed a shower. I had gone running first thing in the morning and then dove into my project. I was sure I was stinky even though I was now wearing deodorant every single day. I took one of my usual too-long showers and no one banged on the door.

Afterward, I wrapped myself in an enormous purple towel and took squeaky-wet steps on the wood floor that led back to my bedroom. I closed my door so I could use the full-length mirror on the other side. I hoped I was not the only girl who occasionally checked herself out. I took a deep breath and dropped the towel. As I stood there, I tried to assess whether I had grown in any important departments. I had just hit one hundred pounds on the scale.

When I told Kate, she said, "I was one hundred pounds when I was nine."

Kate was still bugging me about taking Bet's video off the Web site. I tried to tell her that no one could see her name in the Fat or Not book unless they paused on that exact frame and really studied it. But she wasn't giving up. Kate had talked with her mom and her doctor and was relieved to learn she didn't need to go on a diet. But she was trying not to gain weight, so she "ate more thought-fully," as she put it. This made me laugh because I thought this sounded like she was being thoughtful to her food. "Excuse me, Mr. Apple, let's get you a nice shower before I dry you off and eat you!"

But it actually meant that she wasn't automatically eating dessert every night or sitting in front of the TV or computer with a bag of salty chips. I did this plenty, which Kate said was unfair because I was still a string bean. But at least I was a hundred-pound string bean now.

When I looked at myself, I was a little shocked. My breasts were looking more real in size and shape. And I saw continued changes down below, too. I knew both of these were steps toward getting my period. When I really pressed for nitty-gritty details, the school nurse said that a girl's first period can be predicted—sort of.

She said we could talk more about it and that gave me a BRILLIANT idea: The PLS could give girls a quiz about their signs and symptoms and predict when they would get their periods. I thought we could even charge money for it! I would certainly have paid. We would be kind of like fortune tellers. It was brilliant because "When will I get my period?" was still one of our most asked questions.

I wanted to get to work right away, but I had learned something about teamwork from the whole fiasco with Bet's video. If I wanted to make a big change, I needed to discuss it first with Kate and Piper.

Twenty-three

During our PLS meeting in the school basement, Piper demonstrated the video surveillance powers we now had. Mrs. Percy had come through and said she and Ms. Russo would keep an eye on the library, too. They'd watch in the before- and after-school hours—as time allowed. I was eager to talk about my Period Predictor idea, but I waited patiently.

It was cool that we could, from our secret meeting location, spy on people in the library. There were several views of the library on different squares of the screen. I saw Mrs. Kelbrock sitting at the main checkout desk. And I think I saw Taylor Mayweather file by. It was study hall, after all.

But after about three minutes of watching the library, I wondered how we'd ever catch the bookmark bandit.

I made a mental note to talk with Mimi Caritas, Clem's sister, since she was in the library club. She was in the library so much, she might know something. And she'd probably love to help an eighth-grader. The most recent message we'd received actually mentioned the bookmark campaign.

Attention, PLS: I have boxes of bookmarks and there's no stopping me.

"What are the chances," I said, "that one of us will be watching when the person strikes again?"

"It would be, like, a full-time job," Piper said.

"Teamwork," Kate said. "We could all take shifts."

"Speaking of teamwork, I have a new idea to propose," I said.

I gave them my Period Predictor idea, beaming with pride that I had thought of it.

"Gosh, that's an amazing idea," Kate said.

"How much do you think girls would pay for this?" Piper asked.

"Hellooo, we can't charge money. It's our job to be helpful," Kate said.

"We could charge a small fee and still be helpful," Piper said.

We agreed that I'd work out the details after my talk with the school nurse and Piper could figure out the technical part. We'd talk later about the money issue, but I could see that Kate would never go for it. I chose this moment to spring some good news on her.

"Kate, guess what? Bet figured out how to disguise your name in that video."

"What do you mean?"

I explained how Bet came up with a solution that would mask the names in the Fat or Not book. She didn't have to take down the whole thing. She would just pixelate the frames that featured the pages of the book, where Kate's name was, for an instant, visible. The names would look all wavy and unreadable.

I imitated Bet for the girls: "It's probably better from a privacy standpoint anyway."

Whatever that meant. I was just so happy that I could keep both of my friends happy. Bet would have really been crushed if she couldn't post her *You Bet!* videos on our site. She already had a whole plan for what would go up next. I could tell Kate was relieved.

"Oh, a million thank-yous, Jemma," she said.

After we crept back up the stairs, Kate grabbed my elbow. I thought she was going to thank me again.

"So what's the latest on you and Forrest? You haven't said anything about him in forever."

Her question startled me speechless. It took a while for me to remember that at least to the outside world, he was my boyfriend. It would have been normal for me to talk about him from time to time. But I had nothing to say. Or, rather, there was nothing I *could* say about him and this whole crazy situation.

"It's all good," I said, smiling a tight smile.

Twenty-four

You are a link in a pink chain. Do you know the explorer, Sally Ride? Ride, born 1951, was the first woman to be sent into outer space. Far out!

I was glad to see we had finally entered a more recent century with these e-mails. I read them a little more closely now that I knew who was sending them. Mrs. Percy did not become some warm and fuzzy presence overnight. But I was happy to know such a formidable woman was on our side. I tried to imagine myself as an astronaut. Scary, but wow, what a view.

The most wonderful time of the year inspired a holiday-themed dinner and a movie. It was at Clem's house again because her parents were among the most tolerant.

Mr. and Mrs. Caritas always retired to their bedroom when we arrived. After taking coats and saying hellos, it was rare to see them hanging around. When you're thirteen, that's exactly the amount of parental contact you'd like to have when your friends are over.

Clem and Beau made a modified Christmas dinner. There was turkey and mashed potatoes and Christmas cookies for dessert. The house smelled warm and wonderful and put me in a holiday mood. I was doubly jazzed for both Christmas and the upcoming wedding.

Looking back on this second dinner and a movie night, I can see that I was overexcited and revving too high. For one thing, I was talking a little faster than usual. I seriously couldn't stop myself. I was just so happy to be there, happy I'd be sitting next to Forrest at the table, and happy to be spending the evening at what was nearly a grown-up dinner party. We didn't need to go out again in the cold because Clem decided our movie would be old Christmas specials that she had downloaded.

"I hope you like turkey," I told Forrest, and he laughed. I was not about to fall for the same trick he pulled last time with the pad thai.

I said the food was amazing, which started a domino-effect of more compliments from other people. Clem basked in the praise.

"Clem could have her own cooking show," Beau said.

"I totalllyyy could," Clem cooed.

I looked at her and wondered what it was like to be her. I tried to imagine owning that face and that body and being paid good money just for someone to take pictures of me. Frankly, it was easier to imagine myself hurtling through space like Sally Ride.

"Who wants cleanup duty?" Clem called out when everyone was stuffed.

Unable to stop myself, I said I would do it. Forrest, feeling the pressure, said he would help me. Everyone cleared the table of dishes, bowls, and glasses and went to get started on the movies. First up was *The Grinch*.

The kitchen, unlike the candlelit dining room, was an utter disaster. The big roasting pan that held the turkey was brown with baked-on grease and full of bones and turkey goo. Potato skins sat in heaps on the countertop and the sink was full of dishes Clem and Beau had used in their prep work.

"Great idea, Jem. I'd rather be washing dishes than watching *The Grinch* with my friends," Forrest said.

I turned to face the mountain of dishes in the sink and started sudsing and rinsing them.

"I'm sorry. I was just trying to help Clem, since she made all this stuff. You don't have to clean up if you don't want to," I said.

"Okay," Forrest said bluntly.

I got into a rhythm at the sink so it took me a while to realize he had gone. He just left me alone in the kitchen, like Cinderella. But what could I do? I would look freakish if I just wandered back into the family room. And I couldn't exactly go tell him to get back in here, like I was his mom.

A real boyfriend would have stayed. He might have put on some music, blown into the soap bubbles so they sprayed on me, or even taken the opportunity to kiss me in the privacy of a foreign kitchen. But the reality was that Forrest was just my forever crush—not a boyfriend. And right now, in the quiet of Clem's kitchen, I was thinking that he wasn't even that great of a friend.

I heard the swinging door creak and spun around hoping that Forrest had returned. But it was Clem's sister, Mimi. This time she was in regular pink flannel pajamas, not a tutu.

"Are there any cookies left?" she said. "I like the snowmen with white icing."

I found the tin of cookies for her and she poured a glass of milk.

"Why are you in here alone?" Mimi asked.

The question caught me off guard. I couldn't say the truth and I was getting tired of lying all the time.

"My boyfriend was helping me but he left."

"Boyfriend" stuck in my throat like a bone. Even when I tried not to lie, I lied.

"I don't want a boyfriend," Mimi said.

"No?" I said, "You don't have a crush on anyone?"

"No," she said. "Boys are gross."

"Yeah, I used to think that, too. But then something happens and some of them aren't gross anymore."

In fact, one of them is so not gross that I think about him all the time.

"I can help you," Mimi said. "I know how to load the dishwasher."

So we worked together, efficient as sisters, until the kitchen was clean. I even wiped off every countertop. Then I turned off the overhead lights and switched on the light over the stove, like a nightlight, just like my mom did.

Back in the family room, everyone was gathered in two-somes, except for Forrest. This wasn't exactly a makeout party, but everyone looked really cozy. I sat near Forrest but not super-near him. He hardly looked up when I came in. Moments later he stood up and walked out. Bathroom. I took it as my opportunity. I followed him and waited a polite distance from the door. As I stood in the hallway, a door down the hall inched open and I saw a sliver of light. I prayed it wasn't Mr. or Mrs. Caritas. I was having a bad time but I didn't want to break the spell that we were having an adult-free party. It was Mimi again.

"Hey, Mimi," I said, "C'mere."

I had forgotten to ask her about library club and the bookmark bandit.

She widened her door. "Clem says I can't come out."

"Just for a minute."

She approached me and I asked if she was in library club.

"Uh-huh."

"I thought so. This is kind of secret, but I wanted to know if you ever saw anything unusual at library club— like someone putting bookmarks in some of the books."

"Um, no," she said.

She turned and fast-walked toward her room. I was going to stop her but Forrest opened the bathroom door.

"Forrest, hey. Can I talk to you outside?"

"Why? There's another movie starting. *Peanuts*, I think."

"I just need to."

He followed me to the front porch and I closed the door behind us.

"I'm worried about something," I said.

"What?'

"Well, Piper told me that people are saying stuff about us."

"Like what?"

"That they, um, don't understand why we're a couple. Because you've dated all these, you know, hot girls."

I fake-coughed out of nervousness. He looked at me blankly, so I had to press on.

"People don't believe that you like me. For real, any-way. That's what it sounded like."

"Jem, this is exactly what I'm talking about. All these people always in my business. I'll go out with whoever I want. What does it matter to them?"

"I don't know. I guess I thought you should know that people don't—well, some people might not—believe the act."

"I don't care who believes what. And you shouldn't either."

"So that's it?"

"Yeah."

"Are you going to the wedding?"

"Yeah, we can go together, if you want."

"That's what people—other couples—are doing. You know, it's New Year's and everything," I said.

I was talking to his back now because he had turned to go back into the house. I thought about pulling on the hood of his gray sweatshirt, to stop him like a dog on a leash. I resisted the urge. Forrest pulled on the doorknob but it wouldn't go.

"Jemma, you locked the door."

"I didn't lock it. It must have locked automatically."

"Great, we're stuck out here."

I felt a stab of sadness. First, he left me alone in the kitchen. Then he blamed me for something I didn't even do.

I saw Forrest's hand reach for the doorbell.

"Don't ring the bell! We'll wake up her parents."

"It's freezing. We can't stay out here 'til eleven."

Forrest took me by the elbow and led me out into the yard, aiming for the back of the house, where the family room was. I wish I could tell you he was holding my arm like an escort. But he was clutching my elbow just to steer me this way and that way. It was pitch-black and the ground was unsteady below my feet. I worried about stepping on a wild animal or dog poop. I let Forrest lead me. Step by step, we edged our way around the house, looking for the milky blue light of the TV.

"Birdbath," Forrest said as he helped maneuver us around it.

It took awhile and we went slowly, together, in the dark.

"Patio furniture," he said.

It didn't look like patio furniture. They were shapeless forms shrouded in protective canvas covers. Summer felt a long way off. It was cold enough to snow. Would snowflakes change Forrest's mood? I hoped it would snow at the wedding. Finally, we saw the family room windows on the back of Clem's house and had only to go up and knock.

"Now you have me thinking like they do," Forrest said.

"What?"

"The only good explanation for us to be out here is, you know."

"Oh," I said.

He grabbed my hand and pointed us toward the family room, where there was a patio door. I was cold and my cheeks were flushed, from the cold and/or the conversation. I was trying to make sense of this outdoor adventure and shake out the important parts.

But before I could, Forrest positioned himself between me and the patio door. People could probably see us from inside, I thought. We were standing face-to-face. He looked at me and then I saw his eyes close, his head tilt, and the ever-closer image of his lips coming toward mine. I flinched and then tried to prepare in a nanosecond. I closed my eyes, I tilted my head left, then right, and felt his lips touch mine. He held them there maybe two seconds and pulled back. He smiled at me. My insides melted like marshmallow inside a s'more. I smiled, too. Then Forrest pulled the handle of the patio door.

Piper rushed to the door to let us in.

"Oooh-OOOH-ooh," Piper sang out.

I had a fierce urge to run to the bathroom so I could—I don't know—examine my lips to see if they looked any different. I didn't know what you were supposed to do after you got your first kiss. I was making it up as I went along. I sat down next to Forrest, but not too close.

The girls at the party looked up at us in what I swore looked like jealousy. Forrest McCann had kissed me under a cold, starlit, almost-Christmas December sky. They probably wondered what that felt like. It all happened so fast, I wasn't sure I even knew.

Twenty-five

Ms. Russo made a surprise appearance at Tuesday's Pink Locker Society meeting. This time, we heard her *clomp-clomp-clomp* down the school basement stairs. We were temporarily terrified, but then the shadowy figure edged closer and said, "Yoo-hoo, girls. Don't panic. It's just me."

She pulled up a chair and joined our circle.

"Sorry to interrupt, but I needed to get word to you. Mrs. Kelbrock said she just can't keep ahead of the bookmarks anymore."

"What does that mean? She's just going to let it get out in the open? Principal F. will shut us down in ten seconds flat," Piper said.

"I know, it's frustrating," Ms. Russo said, "but she does

have more to do than sift through all the library books for renegade bookmarks."

"We have to catch the person who's doing it," I said.

"Is that right, Sherlock?" Piper said.

"We're just going to have to get more serious about watching the video surveillance of the library," Kate said. "If they keep showing up, someone's doing it and they could be caught red-handed on that tape."

"Good idea, but may I offer another suggestion?" Ms. Russo said. "This one comes from Mrs. Percy."

Ms. Russo said the two of them talked and she sent a note. Ms. Russo pulled it out of her pocket and cleared her throat.

Dear Girls,

Kudos and laurels for your continued work on the Pink Locker Society! I sympathize with the bookmark issue, but perhaps this is the right moment to allow the PLS to come out in the open. Why spend so much energy trying to hide your light under a bushel basket? Sure, Principal F. may raise a stink, but your supporters are more vast than you know. Then you could forget about the bookmarks. Free speech and all that.

Yours pinkly,
Mrs. Percy

It was intriguing, but also entirely crazy. We'll just let Principal F. and our parents find out and everything will magically turn out fine? I doubted it. I doubted it very much.

"Mrs. P.'s absolutely right," Piper said.

"It does make a certain amount of sense," Kate said.

It was like they read my mind and decided to think the exact opposite.

"You're both completely off track," I said, reminded of the GPS voice on my dad's car.

Kate and Piper turned and looked at me.

"Does anybody except me remember what happened last time?" I said.

I thought back to that awful afternoon, when Principal F. showed up at my house. And I thought about Forrest and how he got dragged into the mess. I cried after everyone left and promised my parents I'd follow the rules. Au revoir, Pink Locker Society.

"I do remember all that, but I think things have changed," Kate said. "We were caught completely off-guard. Now we know what we're doing—and who our friends are."

Kate eyed Ms. Russo, who winked at her.

"Right. I say let the cookie crumble," Piper said. "Just think of how things would be so much better. No more hiding in basements. Maybe we could get our old office back"

"Indeed. I must say I agree," Ms. Russo said. "But it's entirely your decision."

"Principal Finklestein could expel us—or worse," I said. "Can't we at least try to catch the person?"

"Okay, Jem," Piper said. "I guess we can give it one last try."

Twenty-six

Since this was all my idea, I was given the first shift. I had to bring our pink laptop home so I could monitor the library's video surveillance for twenty-four hours. That meant Wednesday after school and all day Thursday. I watched that night until I fell asleep. All was dark and empty by the time evening came. I watched the school janitor make her rounds through the library, thinking for a minute that she was someone with the opportunity. But she touched nothing other than floors and trash cans. Then she turned out the lights and you couldn't see much at all. I doubted the bookmark bandit was sneaking in overnight, so I turned off the laptop and went to bed. Just FYI, watching an empty library on surveillance cam puts you to sleep faster than counting sheep.

I couldn't exactly monitor it during school hours. But I could during study hall since we were all just down in the basement for the PLS meeting anyway. The study hall shift—though the camera showed it was busy in the library—yielded nothing. I watched people take books off the shelf and put them back, but I had to watch with eagle eyes to note if they seemed to insert a bookmark in a book. It appeared no one did.

Kate was on for Thursday. She did as I did, doing what she could from home then checking during study hall. Again, she saw nothing of note. Piper agreed to watch over the weekend.

"This is excrutiatingly boring," Piper said the following week during our PLS meeting. "I don't see how we can keep this up."

Piper explained that she borrowed her mother's smart phone and figured out how to monitor the surveillance from it.

"My mother doesn't understand this phone anyway. It's really too much phone for her," Piper said.

But even with the gift of mobile access, she didn't spot anything or anyone that could help us uncover the bookmark bandit. And if that person kept on spreading the word about the PLS, it would be only a matter of time before we were exposed and, in my opinion, finished for good.

I begged everyone for a few more days, which they granted reluctantly. By Wednesday, Piper wanted to end our failed stakeout.

"Do you really want me to stay home and watch the same boring footage of the library instead of going to the basketball games?" Piper asked.

Friday was the kickoff of the annual boys' basketball tournament. The Candy Cane Tournament, always held the week before Christmas, brought in teams from all over for three nights of basketball. School break was just days away and it was something we looked forward to. Everyone went and watched two games per evening—an approved reason to be out until eleven. We decorated our gym to support Margaret Simon Middle School. *Go Patriots!* Then we spent three nights rooting for them and sitting high in the bleachers in clusters of friends. And boyfriends.

I could not believe Forrest and I had been "dating" for more than a month. Though I had the recent kiss to cling to, our one-month anniversary went by unnoticed. Piper and Kate asked if he got me anything, but I told them that we both thought one-month anniversaries were stupid. I learned that this was the wrong thing to say because Piper and Kate routinely marked these on their calendars and celebrated them with their boyfriends. Now, Christmas loomed. What would I say to explain why Forrest and I didn't exchange gifts—that we thought celebrating Christmas was stupid?

My mom took me, Kate, and Piper to the school gym for the first night of the tournament. We walked in and admired the decorations we had contributed to the decked-out gym. We made giant candy canes to represent each player. We painted them red and white and then used glue and glitter to emblazon the player's number on the candy cane. We cracked ourselves up wondering if the other team would really be intimidated by the thought of facing a team of jumbo peppermint sticks.

"How would a candy cane dribble the ball or shoot?" I wondered aloud.

"I do believe you're underestimating the power of mint, Jemma," Piper said. We laughed so hard, we kind of stumbled into school, three astride.

In the lobby, the school's Christmas tree stood proud in twinkle lights, regular-size candy canes, and basketball ornaments. Forrest wasn't there yet, but Brett was, so Kate ran off to sit with him. Piper was momentarily boyfriend-less, though Dylan would be there as soon as his hockey game was over.

Once we ascended to the top bleacher, our favorite spot, Piper turned to me.

"Jemma, do you and Forrest ever argue? Dylan drives me crazy sometimes."

I knew there was a right answer to this question, but I didn't know what it was.

"No," I said, after a moment's delay. "Not really."

"That's good," Piper said. "It's just weird. You never complain about him and he never complains about you. You're, like, one of the most together couples I've ever met. In eighth grade anyway."

It was a compliment, I knew. But I couldn't take it.

"It's all good," I said, my fallback line.

But just as Piper was praising our month-long relationship, I saw them. Forrest was walking into the gym with Lauren and Charlotte, the Bouchard twins. They were stunningly beautiful twins and each one had him by the arm, like gorgeous bookends with Forrest in between. Forrest was smiling and leaned in close to hear something Lauren said. Or was it Charlotte? From where I sat, I couldn't tell the difference.

I don't know what hit me first. Was it worry that Forrest would soon break up with me to date one of them? Or it might have been anger—anger that he'd so openly flirt with two girls when I was sitting in the very same gymnasium, where I had saved him a seat next to me.

I tried to look away, but kept on staring. I hardly noticed when Kate and Brett sat down in front of me.

"Popcorn?" Kate asked, tilting the cone my way.

When I didn't respond, her eyes followed my gaze to the floor of the gym, where Forrest still stood with both twins. I panicked when I saw all three of them start climbing the bleachers.

He can't be bringing them up here, can he?

My heart lurched again when I realized he wasn't bringing the Bouchard sisters up to where I was sitting. He stopped eight rows below me and the girls sat down on either side of him. I was actually, at that moment, more angry at them than Forrest. Forrest knew we were only in a pretend relationship. But Lauren and Charlotte, on the other hand, knew Forrest had a girlfriend.

I tried to keep my eyes focused on the basketball court, but I mostly watched them. Kate said nothing and I silently thanked her for not drawing attention to the situation. But ten minutes into the game, Piper noticed.

"What the heck, Jem? Why is Forrest down there with the sisty uglers?" It was her flip-flopped term for ugly sisters.

"They're not ugly, Piper," I said.

"Whatever—just trying to make you feel better, girlie. What's the deal down there? Did I speak too soon? Maybe your first fight will be tonight?"

"I don't want to make a scene. They're friends. He can have friends who are girls," I said, faking maturity.

"I know those girls, Jemma. They don't want to be his friends."

I knew it, too.

At halftime, I walked right by, wanting him to see me. He tugged on the sleeve of my sweater. I gave a tight smile to Clem Caritas, who had chosen to join Forrest and his twin girlfriends.

"Hey Jemma, where have you been?" Forrest asked.

"Right behind you, Forrest," I said in an icy tone, and kept on descending the bleachers.

As I passed by them, I had the weird urge to rip down the man-sized candy cane I had painted with the glittery 43 on its back. But then I thought, what did #43 ever do to me? I used the bathroom time to collect my thoughts. I gathered my courage to tell Forrest how this was just unacceptable. I would tell him, not as his girlfriend, but as a friend, that he had hurt my feelings. Who couldn't see how embarrassing this was for me?

But as I took a deep breath and re-entered the gym, Piper caught me.

"Hey, you. Someone's in the library."

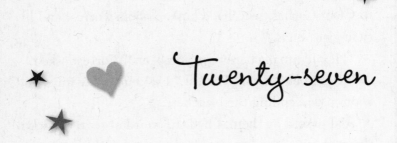

Twenty-seven

Out in the lobby, Kate was waiting for Piper and me. As we walked toward the library, down dark hallways, Piper explained that she never would have checked the library video cameras if Forrest hadn't upset me so.

"I was trying to think of a way to cheer you up, distract you," Piper said.

Before we took off in the library direction, she showed us what she saw on her mother's phone. A small figure working in the dim light of the library with a handful of floppy bookmarks in her left hand.

"Wait," I said. "What are we going to do when we get there?"

"Catch the person," Piper said.

"Jem's right, Piper. It's not like we can arrest whoever it is," Kate said.

"And we can't tell Principal F. That would kind of defeat the purpose," I said.

There we stood outside the closed doors of the library. But we could see inside that there was dim light—was it candlelight?—coming from within the tall shelves.

"You wanted to catch this person and now she is right behind these doors," Piper whispered. "Let's go."

Piper tugged on the door, which made a loud thud as she pulled on it. The bookmark bandit would surely be startled by the noise. We squinted as we looked into the window beside the library doors. The flickering light moved quickly in the direction of Mrs. Kelbrock's office. Kate silently pointed toward the end of the hall and we all quietly race-walked to Mrs. Kelbrock's office door. Her office could be accessed from inside the library or from the hallway.

In the hallway, red EXIT signs illuminated long corridors of dusky gray-black. We rounded the corner and faced Mrs. Kelbrock's office. A sliver of light shone along the floor beneath the door. My heart was thump-thumping in my chest and my mind ran away with itself. I started thinking anyone could be in there—a green-faced monster, an ax murderer, Principal F. himself.

Then the light under the door clicked off. The sliver of light disappeared and we were left in the clinging darkness. Again, my mind raced in crazy directions. How much time had passed? What if the game had ended and my mother was sitting alongside the curb outside of school right now, waiting for me?

It was Piper who reached for the doorknob. I grabbed the back of her sweater but she kept moving forward. She turned the knob slowly and inch by inch pushed open the door. Mrs. Kelbrock's office was small but cheerful, decorated with posters that said things like "Read your heart out!" and "Readers become thinkers." But in the dark, we could see none of that, just the greenish glow of her computer's screensaver.

"We know you're here," Kate said in a wavering voice.

"Come out now and we won't call the police," Piper said.

I looked at Piper and saw her shrug her shoulders as if to say, "It's all I could think of."

The room was perfectly still and quiet, but inside the library, we saw a tiny flicker of light. What if this person had a candle and, because of our pursuit, he or she dropped it and burned down the whole school?

We moved quickly through Mrs. Kelbrock's office and into the library, where we tracked the flickering light to the reference section. Then we heard footsteps and the light moved to nonfiction, where I knew the Dewey decimal numbers went from 000 (generalities) to 900 (geography).

"Just give up already," Piper said.

That made the footsteps and light move even quicker than before. I thought I heard a word or just a whimper. Then we watched the back of a figure return to Mrs. Kelbrock's office. We scurried behind and, again, saw nothing in the office. But Kate pointed to the floor and we saw it. A faint light was coming from under Mrs. Kelbrock's desk. Piper ran her hand along the wall and found the switch. Immediately, the room was flooded in regular, school-day fluorescent light. We saw the toes of two pink sneakers peeking out from under the desk. It was a girl.

Kate leaned down under the desk and said, gently, "Oh my, Mimi."

Kate extended her hand and helped Mimi Caritas get to her feet. She looked scared like she had been crying but now was just staring at us.

"I was just looking for a book," she said in a quiet voice.

Piper knelt down where Mimi had been, under the desk, and pulled out a stack of anti-PLS bookmarks. "Stop the PLS," "PLS = X-Rated," and—a new one— "Pink STINKS."

"Why are you doing this?" Piper asked.

"Did someone make you do this?" Kate asked.

Mimi said nothing.

I stood there trying to piece this together in a way that

made sense. Mimi was the bookmark bandit. Sweet Mimi, who twirled in her tutu and helped me with the dishes?

"Guys, can you give me a minute alone with Mimi?"

Kate and Piper hesitated, then walked back into the empty library, leaving us together.

"Why don't you sit down?" I said, motioning toward Mrs. Kelbrock's green desk chair.

I felt like a police detective with my suspect. Mimi sat but wouldn't look at me. She was staring stiff-necked at her feet.

"You don't like the Pink Locker Society?" I asked.

She shrugged.

"Yes or no?" I asked.

"No."

Progress—at least she was talking.

"How did you know it was me?" she said. "Are you going to tell my parents? Or my sister? Please don't tell Mrs. Kelbrock. I don't want to get kicked out of library club."

"We're not going to tell anyone. Probably not, anyway. We didn't know it was you until tonight," I said.

"Do you know about the Pink Locker Society?" she asked.

"Yes, you could say that. I'm—we're—the PLS. Piper, Kate, and me. We're the ones running the Web site."

"But you guys are so nice," Mimi said, more relaxed now.

"And you made those bookmarks and sent us those messages?"

She nodded.

I thought about everything Mimi had written, including her personal attacks on us. It was hard to connect all that to this scared sixth-grader in front of me. Her feet didn't even touch the floor. She was swinging them now, nervously.

"Why don't we go take the bookmarks out of the books?"

She nodded and guided me over to the fiction section. She pulled out the books and removed more than a dozen bookmarks. She handed them to me, like I was her mother and she was in trouble. Which she was. I told Kate and Piper to go back to the gym.

"I have it under control," I said.

"We'll tell Forrest you're talking to two really hot twin guys," Piper said.

The entire time we'd been tracking down Mimi I had completely forgotten about Forrest. It stung a little—the thought of walking back into that gym and seeing him with Lauren and Charlotte.

After we un-bookmarked the books, I asked Mimi more directly why she had done it. She said it was because the Pink Locker Society Web site made her scared and confused.

"I don't want to wear bras and go out with boys and get the curse and all that other weird stuff."

"Growing up and getting your period is not a curse, Mimi," I said, feeling a little like a big sister.

I had been mystified why she had done all this, but now it started to make a little sense. Other girls had written in to the Pink Locker Society with the same concern. Not a ton of them, but a few. Some said they were embarrassed because they still played with Barbies or because their mom said they needed a bra, but they didn't want to wear one.

It wasn't how I felt; I had always wanted to grow up and seem older. But I could see where a girl might feel this way. Mimi and I locked up the library and started walking toward the gym. I tried to use the time wisely. I told her that she shouldn't call other girls "trashy and cheap."

"That hurt our feelings," I said.

Mimi nodded.

I told her we had to keep the Pink Locker Society a secret to keep it running—even though some people were saying just the opposite. And I told her I wouldn't tell her sister. Then I told her what I knew to be true and she needed to hear most of all—that she wasn't the only one.

"Other girls are scared, too. But it will be okay. Growing up isn't bad and it happens a little at a time," I said.

Mimi had caused us a lot of trouble, but something in me wanted to protect her. I had planned on telling Kate and Piper about Mom being pregnant at the basketball game. But so much had happened now, I couldn't find the energy.

It seemed much longer, but we had lost only an hour to the Mimi situation. The second basketball game had just begun. I caught Mimi's eye a few times back in the gym. I could hardly believe this was the same girl who we pulled out from under Mrs. Kelbrock's desk, the same girl who had been threatening us all this time.

We all felt a sense of accomplishment at having solved the mystery. It helped me not mind—well, at least not as much—that Forrest continued to sit with the Bouchards until very late in the game. When he did decide to join me, I saw Lauren and Charlotte turn around and watch him walk up the bleachers to where I was sitting.

"Nice of you to show up," Piper said.

"Stop, Piper," I said, even though I agreed with her.

Forrest sat alongside me until the game's end. The Patriots won in a squeaker. But I didn't have much to say to him. He didn't even ask where I was the whole time we were involved in the library caper. I wondered if he was seriously interested in Lauren or Charlotte, or both. I wasn't mad exactly. I guess I didn't feel much of anything, which was weird because I was so used to Forrest making me feel a whole lot of something.

Twenty-eight

The next day, we told Ms. Russo, who told Mrs. Percy and Mrs. Kelbrock, that the bookmark bandit had been caught. They were surprised to learn who it was, but as long as she stopped, they promised not to say anything. The day buzzed with holiday anticipation. We were off for the next two weeks, sailing right from Christmas through the New Year and Ms. Russo and Mr. Ford's wedding.

I was so happy to be invited to a real wedding. Most times, only adults are invited. And I was thrilled to have something fun to do on New Year's Eve. Past a certain age, you don't want to be kissing your mom and dad at midnight. Though I was fairly certain I wouldn't be kissing Forrest. I had dreamed of kissing him so many times that I puzzled over our actual kiss. It was fine—a slow and gentle kiss, not a pushy one—but it lacked a certain something.

For the wedding, I had a sparkly silver dress to wear and medium-high heels. For Christmas, Santa gave me some accessories, including a silver clutch handbag to match my dress.

The days following Christmas went slowly. My mother was feeling better. She said, "The second trimester is a dream," which I took to mean she wasn't barfing up her breakfast anymore. I tried to be helpful and to keep busy. I went for runs most days and I made time for relatives and friends. I had sleepovers with Kate and Piper. One afternoon, I met Bet for tea. Again, I was tempted to just unload my backpack of untruths on her, but I'd been lying so long about Forrest, I couldn't quite form the words.

I found out what was worse than Forrest not getting me any Christmas gift. It was Forrest not getting me a present but asking me to tell people that he did. He stopped me at my locker before school let out for the holidays and asked me to tell everyone that he had given me a gift certificate to the Tuscan Oven.

"No one will know if we actually went to dinner," he said. "Cool?"

"Sure, fine," I said.

"People will ask what *you* got me," he said. "What should I say?"

"Tell them I made you a huge batch of your favorite Christmas cookies."

"What kind?"

"All sorts, but double batches of iced gingerbread and peanut butter chocolate chip."

"That sounds incredible. You didn't actually do that, did you? 'Cause that would be awesome," he said.

"No, maybe next year," I said, smiling a little. It was the first time I let myself enjoy anything about him in weeks.

" 'Kay," he said. "I'll call you about the wedding. To set up rides."

"Yep," I said. "Merry Christmas."

"Same to you, Jemma."

I would be lying if I said I didn't think of him on Christmas. Christmas Eve to be exact. It's just one of those nights that stands out among the rest and makes you wish you were with the people that matter most to you. I love my family, don't get me wrong, but how cool would it be to spend Christmas Eve with your crush, especially if your crush liked you back?

I pictured myself at Gibraltar with Forrest and something inside me slammed on the brakes. It had always been so easy to imagine Forrest and me and everything working out beautifully. But for more than a month, I had tried the experiment. We'd spent time together. We'd talked more than ever before. He'd held my hand and put his arm around me at the movies. Forrest had even kissed me. But he didn't fall madly in love with me. If it hadn't happened during all this time, would he ever?

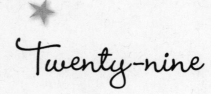

Twenty-nine

9:45 a.m.
14 hours and 15 minutes until midnight

New Year's Eve stands out among all other days in the calendar because of the big countdown. From the moment you wake up on December 31, the whole day is just tick-tocking away. I love when midnight gets close enough that the hour and minute countdown is inset in the corner of the TV screen. Sometimes I have a friend over to watch the ball drop, but usually it's Chinese food, sherbet punch, and then a midnight cheer with Mom and Dad. Next year, it would be me, Mom, Dad, and a baby to be named later.

But that was 365 days away. Tonight, I'd be counting

down to the new year at Ms. Russo and Mr. Ford's wedding reception. What a beautiful relief it was to have somewhere really fun to be on this party night of all party nights. And at midnight, how mind-blowing would it be to have a boy kiss me at three—two—one, Happy New Year!!??

The anticipation was brutal as I lay in bed with the covers still tucked beneath my chin. I thought time would move faster if I forced myself back to sleep even for a little bit. When I did get up, I hoped my zebra-striped fuzzy slippers were in reach. It had snowed two days before—right between Christmas and New Year's—and it was icy cold outside. A waste of snow, I thought, because we were already off from school.

My silvery dress was hanging on my bedroom door, my new silver purse dangling from my doorknob. Could you wear too much silver to a winter wedding? I hoped not as I had metallic dressy sandals and planned to wear dangling silver snowflake earrings. Piper's mom once taught me this fashion rule: Always take off one accessory before leaving the house. It was supposed to prevent you from "overdoing it." But I wasn't willing to forgo any of my silver items.

My happy dress-up thoughts were quickly overshadowed by more worrisome Forrest-related thoughts. What if he spent all his time with the Bouchard sisters, just like he did at the holiday basketball tournament? I pictured

Lauren and Charlotte on either side of Forrest, each kissing one of his cheeks.

I knew I shouldn't be worried, since we were going to the wedding as dates. We planned to go together just like the other couples we knew. Piper and Dylan would be there, but Kate and Brett were no longer a pair. Just before Christmas, Brett had broken it off because he "wanted to see other people." (At least this excused Kate from the boyfriend Christmas gift obligation.)

Kate briefly worried that Brett may have broken up with her because of the Fat or Not list, but I assured her that could not be it. She said she still liked Brett and was a little sad, but had also confessed that hanging out with him so much had gotten a little dull. In a way, she told Piper and me, she wished she had the courage to end the relationship first. But Kate didn't want to hurt Brett's feelings.

"It's better to be the dumper than the dumped," Piper always told us. But so far none of us had taken her advice.

Thirty

11:30 a.m.
11 hours and 30 minutes until midnight

I finally woke up and found my fuzzy slippers. In the kitchen, I saw that Mom had already given me one of her dreaded chore lists. She liked to write them on index cards and even put a box next to each one so I could check off my progress. The list began with "put laundry away" and ended with "help undeck the halls." I never liked returning the Christmas ornaments and decorations to the sad cardboard boxes and plastic tubs. Outside, my father was already unwinding the twinkly white Christmas lights from the shrubs and door frame. I protested that it was too early to take down the lights.

"It's supposed to snow again tonight," he said. "And I don't want your mom out here on this ladder."

With a baby on the way, Dad had become more protective of Mom. It was sweet. In recent weeks, he didn't want her bringing in the heavy groceries, crawling into the storage closet, or getting into arguments with me. I exchanged sparks with Mom from time to time, which he seemed to tolerate before, but no longer. Mom had invited me to help design the nursery for the baby. It took all my strength not to paint it pink, pink, pink. But Mom said, "What if it's a boy?" Yikes. What if?

When I was outside talking to Dad, I was surprised at how warm it was despite the four inches of snow on the ground. Everything remained coated in white except the roads, which were black and wet. The sun felt warm on my back through the fleece jacket I was wearing. I decided to go for a pre-lunch run. It got me (temporarily) out of my chores. I thought it might calm my high-strung mood and help pass the many hours I had ahead of me before I could start getting ready for the wedding.

I listened to the squeak-crunch of my sneakers on the wet ground. My breathing quickened but it was even and I felt like I wanted to keep going. I probably could have kept on running for hours with the shining sun overhead and the air cold enough to chill the back of my throat. I did not run in the direction of Forrest's house. I actually tried to put him out of my mind. It almost worked.

Bzzz-Bzzz. It was my phone vibrating on my hip. I stopped near a square-shaped park with a gazebo in the middle. The grass was still snow-covered, but the criss-crossing pathways were clear.

"Jemma?" Piper said. "I am so upset I can't even speak."

"Well, you are speaking."

"No time for jokes. Dylan just broke up with me."

"Oh, Pipes."

"This has never happened to me before IN MY ENTIRE LIFE," she said.

This made me feel sad for her but it also irritated me just a tad. Piper had already had more than a dozen supercute boyfriends. Literally none of them had ever broken up with her.

"Well, what did Dylan say?"

"He said, 'It's not you. It's me.'"

"What *about* him?" I asked.

"That's just it. I don't know either. He dumped me in a text."

"Cold."

"I know. And my phone was charging so I didn't even see it until hours later. He already changed his Facebook status to 'single.'"

"Well, first things first. You're still going to the wedding, right?"

"Yes, I'm going. And I'm going to look amazing. But

I'll be alone tonight. Just like Kate. Jem, you're the only one with a date for New Year's."

Oh, Piper. I am more alone than you realize.

"We'll all hang out—the three of us. We'll have a great time. I'm sure of it," I said as I walked through the melting park.

"No offense, but I hope everyone doesn't get all coupled off. It's going to be a romantic wedding after all. With slow dancing," Piper said.

I assured her we'd all stick together and reminded her that Bet would be there, too. She was the official videographer for the wedding. Ms. Russo wanted a video record of the event, but was trying to avoid the "wedding industrial complex" and not spend too much money. Bet offered to do it for free—her wedding gift to the happy couple.

Thirty-one

I worked fast, accomplishing both my shower and the chores, which included undressing the Christmas tree. Then it seemed like a good time to polish my nails. Once I finished with the silver polish I spread out on the couch. There's not much to do while you are waiting for nail polish to dry. You can't read a book or straighten your hair or eat an orange. You just have to sit and wait. I had forgotten to turn on the TV in advance, so I just lay there waiting.

My parents must have sensed my availability, because that's when they pounced. Both of them came in and sat on either side of me—Mom on the reclining chair and Dad on the love seat. They were looking at me so intently I got worried. Had something happened to Grandma or Donald Hall, my cat? Were they about to say I wasn't allowed to go to the wedding? Had they found out about the Pink Locker Society?

Nope, it was none of the above. They just wanted to check in about the baby.

"It's going to mean big changes for all of us, Jemma," Mom said, putting her hand on my shoulder.

"But you'll always be our Cupcake," Dad said.

Enough with calling me Cupcake, I told them. But I also said I was getting used to the idea that the baby was coming and I was happy—happy! Was it wrong to wish for a girl, I wondered.

"It'll be great," I said, meaning it mostly.

They said they were glad to hear it, and left me alone with my drying nails.

I felt a little strange keeping the baby a secret from my friends for all these weeks. But truth be told, that wasn't the biggest secret I'd been keeping. Forrest kept entering my thoughts as I got ready for the wedding. I wanted to find the courage to talk to him tonight, *really* talk to him.

Once dressed, with my hair straightened and all my silver on, I felt good. I decided not to wear hose because panty hose is so very old ladyish. But no hose is quite cold when it's New Year's Eve, so I put on a pair of black leggings. This was done for warmth, but looked kind of high fashion, I thought.

The only trouble was they were footless leggings, so my feet and toes were still exposed to the winter chill. But with thoughts swirling around my head like a blizzard, cold toes were the least of my worries.

Thirty-two

5:25 p.m.
6 hours and 35 minutes until midnight

Kate's mom picked up me and Piper. Mrs. Parker insisted on taking some photos before she dropped us off at Gibraltar.

"I can't help myself. You girls look like movie stars," she told us as she parked along the curb.

Standing outside Gibraltar's stone walls, I thought it didn't feel so bad. My silvery toes were pleasantly chilled. I wondered if Forrest was already there. I wondered, too, if it would be another evening of me watching him chat up the Bouchard twins.

The camera flash lit up the snow-dusted stone wall,

where we posed. My mother had told me Gibraltar was once the residence of a Vanderbilt. When the last owner—an elderly woman—passed away, the property fell into disrepair. A group of local horticulturalists brought the garden back to life, but the house remained shuttered and boarded up.

Even in winter, Gibraltar had curb appeal. Upon those stone walls were carved sculptures of chubby, bare-bottomed cherubs and large stone bowls of fruit. It was dusky dark already, so we saw all these features only because Ms. Russo and Mr. Ford had strung white twinkle lights everywhere.

Lights lined the arched entrance to the garden. Inside, more lights dangled off tall trees and draped across the backs of benches set on either side of the aisle. Blue lights clung to the hedges on both sides of the makeshift altar where the happy couple would recite their vows. The wedding was going to be outside, for real, in the winter. The aisle itself, where Ms. Russo would make her grand entrance, was outlined with white lights.

Up a twisting path there was a huge white tent. It glowed like a Japanese lantern in the night and offered hope that we would soon be indoors.

"It's heated," Forrest said when he found me alone. Kate and Piper ran off to get wedding programs. Me and my toes were glad to hear about the warm tent in our future. The ground was cold and hard but clear of snow.

I wiggled my toes in my sandals to ward off frostbite. Much of the snow had melted during the day, but it still clung to the garden's fountains and sculptures, some eroded by years of sitting out in the weather. Spotlights shone dramatically upon smooth Greek goddesses and more chubby cherubs. In summer, the fountains would be alive and splashing but tonight they were just frozen observers of this romantic scene.

I tried not to stare, but Forrest looked amazing in a blue sport coat and tie, like he might have been yachting earlier in the day. Overcome at the sight of him, I told one of my secrets.

"My mom's going to have a baby," I said.

"Seriously?" he asked.

"For real."

Forrest rocked back on his heels and raised his eyebrows. Then he turned and pulled me into a hug. He let me go, put his hands on my shoulders, and looked me straight in the eye.

"Wow, Jem. Awesome," he said, then his hands dropped to his sides again.

"Yeah, I hope it's a girl," I said.

I nodded and we both turned to watch the wedding scene unfolding before us.

"Oh, I'm shocked," Forrest said sarcastically. "I still remember when they told me my mom was going to have Trevor."

"What were you—two years old?"

"Yeah, I have a good memory. I'm glad he was born. He didn't get really annoying until, like, last year."

"You're the first person I told. First friend, I mean."

"Really?" he said.

He was standing near a pair of chimeras, little garden stoves that flickered with orangey-red flames. I imagined what he was feeling at that very moment. I've always liked the pillow of warmth that surrounded campfires, or fireplaces. I tried to stand in the spot where the cold and warmth met. It reminded me of the night Forrest and I talked outside on my back porch, while s'mores cooked on the grill.

It felt like a thousand days since that moment, when he squeezed my hand and first told me of his plan. Not much time had actually passed, but I felt like a different person now.

Having an almost-real boyfriend had changed me. I felt older, probably because that almost-real boyfriend was the love of my life. It was like there were two different Forrests. One I made up in my head when he was only a crush. And the other who was a real guy, who needed a favor from me, who sometimes was nice to me. (He was awfully sweet about the baby.) And sometimes he seemed to not care much one way or the other. You can't go back, my mother likes to say. I guess I couldn't go back to the time when Forrest was just someone exciting to think about. I knew the real Forrest, at least a little, and he knew me.

I had hoped it would inspire in him a genuine love for me, but it hadn't. It was like we were teammates. We had a job to do: pretend to be a couple. We did it and we went on with our separate lives. It was at that moment I made a decision.

Everyone was starting to situate themselves on the bench seats. Kate and Piper found us, handed us both programs, and we took seats that gave us a good view. Those already seated kept looking over their shoulders to see if the bridal party was in view. Just then, the music started playing. Real musicians were seated to the left of the altar. Bows met violins and this fairytale setting now had almost everything.

Thirty-three

$\mathcal{M}$ s. Russo, for weeks, had been complaining about how getting married had become this enormous industry and there were a billion things you needed to buy and services you needed to employ to make it official. She had dropped two Bible-thick bridal magazines on her desk as proof.

She and Mr. Ford pledged to not do things by the official rules. No wedding planners, no special videographer (Bet would do), no expensive location, and no flowers. They would have frozen in the cold anyway, she said. They really did it their way, I thought, as the crowd turned to face the back of the garden. Everyone in the places, Ms. Russo stood at the top of the frozen aisle, her hands warm in a furry white muff (not real animal fur, she told us).

She wore a matching cape with a fur collar. The dress underneath was simple and long-sleeved, made of heavy silk. It skimmed the ground and was tailored to fit. Wedding clothing and accessories were the only extravagances in which she apparently indulged.

Ms. Russo looked very un-teachery tonight. Her long hair was pulled high up on top of her head. The chin-length veil framed her face like a halo as it caught light from the twinkle lights, the lanterns, and all the tall candles. Forrest sat on my left, with Kate, Piper, and Bet on my right. We were on a bench so I was happy to shift a little closer to Kate, for sheer body warmth. My toes had started to suffer. I kept a margin of space between Forrest and me.

Some survival instinct must have kicked in because I started bouncing my feet in a kind of in-place run. It was quiet, thankfully, but the people around me noticed. When Forrest looked down and saw my naked toes, his mouth fell open.

"Aren't you freezing?" he whispered.

He took off his scarf and dropped it on my feet. I had to admit it helped. I tied it snugly around both feet and felt warmth again in my skin, layer by layer. Piper saw the exchange and winked at me.

I gave Forrest a thumbs-up, then tried to refocus on the

ceremony. I didn't want to miss the vows. Weeks ago, Ms. Russo told us that they were using traditional vows, but thankfully, the standard phrasing for the bride was now "love, honor, and cherish" not "love, honor, and obey." No, Ms. Russo would have never stood for that.

But it wasn't yet time for the vows. The white-haired pastor was addressing the about-to-be-married couple with some advice. He said he recommended "three Ps" for a happy marriage: provide, protect, and pursue.

Provide was just helping each other with basic stuff and also providing emotional support. Protect meant more than just moving the person out of the way of a falling rock.

"I mean protect in every sense," he said. "Protect each other by holding each other in high esteem and speaking well of each other, to friends and family, always."

Pursue was the one that got me. Pursue meant exactly what it sounded like. That you should "court" and seek out that other person. I figured it meant doing nice stuff for them or even dressing up and looking good for a date. In other words, you singled out this person as the one you wanted. You made an effort.

I tried to stop myself, but I began measuring Forrest by the standard of the three Ps. Not that we were married or anything. I knew that we were only in eighth grade. It's just that I wished so much that we had the beginning ingredients for something that could someday be that big and important. Giving me his scarf for my cold toes was a kind gesture, but my heart knew it wasn't enough. I had to admit that Forrest had done nothing to pursue me. That was the major missing element. It was why I felt so empty about everything.

For Forrest, this arrangement was convenient. I was a friend, and he probably thought I was a cool girl for agreeing to participate in his plan. But he was not driven in his heart by true feelings for me. And if he kissed me at midnight it would only be because he thought that's what we were supposed to do, for the sake of appearances.

That stood in contrast to what I witnessed in that illuminated garden. Ms. Russo and Mr. Ford turned to each other and took their vows. They held hands and spoke directly to one another. Ms. Russo had trouble getting through her lines. At one point, she raised her hands—palms out—to Mr. Ford. This gesture seemed to hold back a flood of emotion and she was able to finish what she was supposed to say. It was the "for richer, for poorer, in sickness and in health" part. I saw Mrs. Percy, two rows ahead, dab her eyes with a tissue. I was curious to see Mr. Percy, but the person sitting beside her was an older woman.

Mr. Ford said his vows in a clear, steady voice and then the priest announced that these two teachers were husband and wife. They went in for the kiss even before he said to. All of us, the rows of students, family, and friends, broke into glove-handed applause. The newly married couple bounded up the aisle and I saw Bet race in that direction to catch their triumphant march on video. With almost equal vigor, the crowd headed for the winding path that led to the glowing warmth of the tent. Someone had taken an early peek and said it had an ocean of tables and a dance floor.

I stayed seated. I told Kate and Piper to go on ahead and asked Forrest to stay.

"We'll catch up," I said.

"Okay," Kate said, shooting me a smile.

Forrest sat back down on the bench.

"Don't you want to get your feet inside?" he asked. "Warm tent just over there."

"I do, but I wanted to talk to you first."

For a moment, I lost all will to do what I meant to do. I didn't want it to be over, but it already was. In truth, it never started.

"If it's okay with you, I think it would be good, you know, if we went back to normal," I said. I was shocked at the words—my own words.

"What do you mean?" Forrest said, turning to face me.

"I mean stop pretending to be going out, if that's okay with you."

He raised his eyebrows and looked straight ahead at the bench in front of us.

"Um, sure. If it's not cool with you, you know, fine."

"Good," I said. "Thanks."

"I guess this means you'll be going out with someone else now," Forrest said. He sounded a little angry.

"No. There's no one else."

This was painfully true. Still.

"Seriously?" Forrest asked. "I heard Jake liked you."

"He's a nice guy, but no, I'm not dating him."

"So you're just dumping me for no reason?" Forrest asked.

"Can I really break up with you if we were never really going out?" I asked.

I hoped this would make him smile, at least, but he continued to stare at the bench ahead.

"Everyone will say you dumped me," Forrest said.

Once again, Forrest surprised me. I thought he'd be happy to be rid of me, to clear the way for the Bouchard twins.

"Maybe we can tell everyone that it was mutual—that we both agreed to stop seeing each other?"

"I guess," Forrest said. "No one ever believes that."

"I won't say anything bad about you," I said. Forrest turned from the bench and looked at me. My nose was cold and running a little bit, so I rubbed it on the back of my hand.

The crowds had thinned enough by now and the tent on the hill had become a hive of activity. We were nearly alone in the wintry garden.

"You know I bought you a real Christmas gift," he said.

This came out of nowhere.

"What was it?"

"Nothing. It was stupid."

"I don't think it's stupid," I said softly. Suddenly, I was willing to sit here in the cold all night, if we could work this out.

"We should go, right?" he said.

I just looked at him, wordless.

He got up to go and I didn't want to let him get too far ahead.

I stood, grabbed my silver purse, and—*clatter-crash-boom*—I was down. In my hurry, I had forgotten about the scarf. I stood up and tried to take a step but it hog-tied my feet. I went down, like a falling tree. First my right hip, followed by my right elbow, thudded on the seat of the wooden bench.

Forrest heard the commotion and turned around to find me flopped like a silvery mermaid. I quickly unbound my feet and straightened up. I handed Forrest his scarf. He looked at me blankly and said, "Keep it." He offered his hand and pulled me up. Then he let it go. We walked in silence toward the light and the sound of happy voices.

Thirty-four

7:59 p.m.
4 hours and 1 minute until midnight

Kate and Piper were waiting at table 21 for us. When they saw us walk in, they ran over.

"It's four hours until the new year," Kate said.

"Right, I have four hours to find a new boyfriend," Piper said.

Forrest peeled off and walked in the direction of a table of boys who were already eating bread from the baskets. Kate and Piper recorded his presence and his quick passage. They gave me questioning looks

"I have some news—actually, I have bad news and good news. I'm going to start with the bad news."

"That's the best way to do it," Piper said. "What's the bad news?"

"Forrest and I broke up," I said.

Kate clutched her chest and looked alarmed. Piper, too, grimaced as if something tragic had happened.

"I'm okay, I really am. We decided. It was mutual. I didn't dump him and he didn't dump me."

"I don't think you can do that," Piper said.

"Yes, you can, and we did."

"Are you sooooo sad?" Kate asked.

Her kind concern was just too much and tears sprang to my eyes. Kate immediately hugged me. I pulled back and finally explained.

"Forrest was never my real boyfriend," I said. "It was a favor I did for him."

"What kind of favor?" Piper asked.

"I pretended to be his girlfriend so he could get a break from dating," I said.

"OMG, Jemma. You wrote in to the PLS," Kate said.

"Yes," I said. "I'm finally taking your advice. I'm really sorry for lying."

"I can't believe he asked you to do that," Piper said. "Why did you break up with him if you're so in love with him?"

"I didn't break up with him, remember? We both agreed," I said, feeling guilty about this white lie.

Piper stared at me so intently that I broke.

"Piper, the only thing worse than *not* knowing if your crush likes you is knowing that he doesn't," I said.

"Forrest likes you," Piper said. "He put his arm around you at the movies. He was always laughing and making jokes with you. I saw him kiss you!"

"One time. He never sang a song for me," I said. It was kind of a dig because I knew Forrest sang for Piper once. But that wasn't the point.

"Okay, he liked me but he didn't like me–like me," I said. We all knew the difference between a single like and a double like.

"Gawd, girls, we are all single. Can you believe it?" Piper said.

"What a way to start the new year," Kate said.

Thirty-five

9:38 p.m.
2 hours and 22 minutes until midnight

The wedding tent was as elegant as any place I'd ever been. A chandelier hung over the dance floor of black and white tiles. A big buffet table offered silver tray after silver tray of fancy food. Little blue canisters of flame kept everything warm from underneath. We were seated in a sea of round tables covered in white tablecloths. We had assigned seats, which apparently is how they do it at weddings. We all had been given little cards with our names and table numbers on them.

But what we hadn't expected was that Forrest, Brett, and Dylan were also assigned to table 21. It was sweet of

Ms. Russo to create this little group of couples. How was she to know all three couples were now kaput? She and Mr. Ford popped by the table during a tour of the room. They were as cheerful as daisies.

"Thank you all for coming. It means the world to us that our students wanted to come," Ms. Russo said.

"We'll always remember you being here," Mr. Ford said.

But when they moved on to the next table of guests, the mood dipped. Piper sulked a little, still miffed at Dylan for breaking it off with her. Dylan, for his part, stared into his plate. Brett and Kate made conversation, not with each other, but with others at the table. Forrest was quiet. He didn't look at me, and—like Dylan—mostly focused on eating.

"Hey, I wonder if they're serving pad thai," I said, trying to revive an old joke, a shared story.

Forrest didn't react and the others didn't either. They had no idea what I meant. The near silence at our table gave me plenty of time to think about the ungiven Christmas gift. What was it and did it mean he might like me—like me after all?

Dinner was not pad thai, it was roast chicken. We were hungry, so the table chatter all but disappeared as we ate. None of us reached for the disposable camera in the center, meant for candid photos of the tablemates.

Just seeing Ms. Russo and Mr. Ford together was a lift

though. I watched them float around the room, greeting guests. They were introduced to wild applause before dinner. Then they danced to "What a Wonderful World," the same old song the DJ played the night of the Backward Dance, when Mr. Ford proposed from the stage. We all toasted them with some bubbly. Not champagne for us, but at least it was sparkling grape juice.

It was a relief when dinner was over. Forrest quickly exited to hang out with his friends. Mrs. Percy took the mic after dinner and said the wedding cake would be cut a little later. Kate, Piper, and I spent the next couple of hours dancing to nearly every song, except the slow ones, of course. Bet put down her video camera and danced with us for awhile, too. We all took breaks only to get water or more sparkling juice. Finished with her sulking, Piper had no trouble being single. She was asked to dance nearly every time the music slowed for couples. Kate and I clung together during those times. It was then that she told me her secret.

"Jemma, I feel so terrible, but I have something to admit," she said.

"Kate, compared to the Forrest thing, how bad could it be?"

"Well, remember when the PLS got that question about the Fat or Not list?" Kate said.

"From Emma Shrewsberry?"

"It wasn't from Emma," Kate said. "It was from me."

I was immediately pleased for Emma, but sad for Kate.

"I can't believe that. You were really that worried about your weight?" I asked.

"Yes, Jemma. I wish you understood."

I let some silence pass between the two of us. As well as you know your best friend, you don't know everything.

"I feel better about things now because I'm eating better and stuff," Kate said. "I just wanted you to know."

I could tell she was embarrassed. I immediately knew what would make her feel better.

"Well, now we're even. We both wrote in to the PLS for answers," I said.

She smiled at me. Then we both noticed that the music sped up again and the couples were breaking apart.

Before we could get up, Piper dropped herself into the folding chair between Kate and me.

"I wonder if Piper has something to confess, too," Kate asked me.

"What are we confessing?" Piper said.

"Nothing," I said, enjoying this little secret between two best friends.

Thirty-six

For a while, we had only our cell phones to help us count the hours and minutes until midnight. Then our school basketball coach took the mic and explained that he was setting up a portable scoreboard clock for the countdown. He also announced that wedding cake was available. A throng of guests, mostly eighth-graders, moved across the wooden floor to grab the first slices from the dessert table.

I had been occasionally tracking Forrest's movements during the reception. We hadn't had any direct contact since dinner, but now I wondered if he'd return to our table to eat cake. I saw him in line ahead of us with Brett and Dylan.

I purposefully didn't look in his direction. I wasn't trying to be mean, it's just that I thought I would never get over him if I didn't change my old patterns. Though I had brought it on myself, I was still getting used to the idea that we were no longer a fake couple. I enjoyed my "in a relationship" status and wondered how long it would be before I felt normal as my single self.

"Girls, girls, there's someone I'd like you to meet," Mrs. Percy said.

"But we were just getting some cake," I said as she pulled us out of line.

"Oh, we have the inside track on the cake. We'll get you some right after," Mrs. Percy said.

Mrs. Percy put her arms around us and guided us to her table. She was almost unrecognizable tonight in a periwinkle blue dress that sparkled—nothing like the all-business clothes she wore behind the front counter of the principal's office. Seated at table 7 was the same woman who'd been sitting next to Mrs. Percy at the wedding ceremony. She wore a lavender pantsuit with a scarf wrapped around her neck in a glamorous way. Large pearl earrings accessorized her look.

The lavender lady smiled at us and started right in.

"Oh—I am so pleased to meet you. Just tickled! Please sit down."

"Girls," Mrs. Percy said, "This is my sister, Edith. My *older* sister."

"Oh, thanks a lot, Addie," she said.

I looked at Kate and Kate looked at me and we both looked at Piper. This was *Edith*! Edith—who had first told us we were now members of the Pink Locker Society. Though we only knew her as a voice on the phone, she helped us set everything up and provided that beautiful, newly refurbished office behind our pink locker doors.

"I don't even know what to say," Piper said (and it was rare for Piper to be speechless).

"It's so nice to finally meet you," Kate said.

"Yeah," was all I could contribute.

"I just wanted you to know how proud I am of the way you pulled yourselves up by your bootstraps," Edith said.

"You're not mad at us?" Piper said.

"Mad? Oh heavens, no. I'm sorry you've had to face such . . . such difficulties," Edith said with a wary look around the room.

"Tell them what you want to do, Edith," Mrs. Percy said.

"Oh, yes. Well, I think it's just dreadful that you're meeting in that awful basement. And it's dreadful, too, that you have had to skulk around like criminals," Edith said. "I say let's get you back in your beautiful office and let's get the whole PLS out in the open."

"I agree with Edith. That whole bookmark affair was just a waste of everyone's time," Mrs. Percy said.

I said I didn't want everyone to know I was in the PLS and that we met behind the pink locker doors.

"Oh, of course, dear," Edith said. "Your identities can remain a secret, and your office must remain a secret. But the PLS exists. Why shouldn't everyone know that?"

We all sat there a moment, happy and questioning and a little stunned.

"No need for immediate action tonight—it's a party," Mrs. Percy said. "Let's reconvene when school gets back into session."

"Agreed!" Edith said.

Then Mrs. Percy told us to "sit tight." She and Edith disappeared and returned with slabs of white chocolate raspberry mousse cake for each of us. Then they left again and returned with small, steaming cups of tea. It seemed like the fanciest, most grown-up dessert I had ever eaten.

Earlier, Bet had captured Ms. Russo and Mr. Ford on video. They sliced into the cake with a fancy ribboned knife and then sweetly fed each other bites. When Edith and Mrs. Percy returned to the table, they handed us each an extra slice wrapped in a paper wedding napkin.

"For under your pillow," Mrs. Percy said.

This made absolutely no sense to any of us.

"You don't know about that?" Edith asked. "You put the cake under your pillow and you'll dream about the person you're going to marry."

"A silly old tradition, but you never know," Mrs. Percy said.

I wondered if that meant I would dream of Forrest that night. The band struck up another slow tune—no words— but I could pick up on the melody enough to know it was about leaving your heart in San Francisco. I felt a little like I'd left my heart on that bench outside in the winter garden. But I also felt like I had ripped off a bandage. Better to have done it quickly so I could move on.

Thirty-seven

11:58 p.m.
2 minutes until midnight

Hardly anyone, except a few dullsville teachers, left the wedding early. Why not stick around for the big moment? Balloons, confetti, noisy party horns, and silly hats had been provided. I felt increasing tension as the moment approached. I didn't want to be anywhere near Forrest at midnight for fear of the awkwardness. And I didn't want to see him get any Happy New Year hugs or kisses from anyone else.

Piper felt the same way about Dylan, so she and Kate and I agreed we'd hug each other at midnight and then scoot directly outside together.

"Jemma still hasn't told us her good news," Kate said.

"I completely forgot about that," Piper said.

"At midnight, I'll tell," I said.

Inside the tent, it was hard to navigate because so many people positioned themselves on the dance floor to have a clear view of the countdown clock. At one minute, I really started to feel nervous inside. The seconds ticked off so quickly and before I knew it, my two best friends and I were arm in arm counting, "Three, two, one . . ."

"Happy New Year!"

The crowd erupted. It wasn't quite Times Square, but it sure felt like it to us. Confetti was flying, balloons were dropping, and horns were blowing. The band immediately started playing "Auld Lang Syne," heavy on the saxophone. The three of us weaved our way through the crowd, picking up a hug here or there, until we finally had a clear path and were again outside in the quiet winter night.

"Let's find a falling star and wish on it," Kate said.

We looked up at the sky together. What I would wish for, I had no idea. Then suddenly, I knew. It was the perfect wish for a night of new beginnings.

"I know you're not supposed to tell people what you wish for, but I'm going to tell you," I said.

"Please let it not involve a boy," Piper said, "I'm just about done with boys."

"Yeah, right. We'll remind you about that at *your* wedding," Kate said.

"What I'm wishing for is that, in five months, I will be the big sister to a healthy, wonderful baby," I said.

Kate and Piper reacted as if I'd just won an Olympic gold medal. There was hugging and screaming and more hugging and I started to cry. They were not sad tears or purely happy tears, because I was still unsure about everything. But they were, for sure, hopeful tears.

Our conversation erupted in a million different directions. They said I'd be a great big sister and there were jokes about diaper changing. They said they'd help me babysit. Then we marveled over meeting Edith and the excitement we shared for the next pink step we would take together.

"Viva la babies!" Piper said, blowing her party horn.

"Viva la big sisters!" Kate called out, punching her fist in the air.

It was my turn. I stood on a bench for dramatic effect, even though it was hard to hoist myself up there in my silver dress and heels.

"Viva la best friends forever!"

Ask the PLS
Pink pearls of wisdom from our Blog

In just a short time, the Pink Locker Society has received 30,000 questions from girls. Here are some of the best questions and best answers from the army of Pink Locker girls out there!

Overweight and Unhappy
Today's question is a tough one.

> *Dear Jemma:*
>   *I am overweight and I don't know what to do. People make fun of me.*
>
>> *Signed,*
>> *Anonymous*

I get pretty upset thinking about people making fun of our friend. Though we have some control over the way we look, it's very hard when people criticize you for something like body shape. Here's my best advice for her:

1. **Get help figuring out if you are actually overweight.** You can get an idea by using a BMI calculator. It can help to have a parent help you with this. Don't panic if your BMI score puts you in the overweight category. It's just a piece of information that will help you, your parents, and your doctor figure out what to do next.

2. **Talk to your doctor.** If you are not at a healthy weight, your doctor can suggest steps to take. And if your weight is OK, your doctor can tell you that, too.

3. **Know you are not alone.** Kids can't do it alone when it comes to eating healthy and getting enough exercise. Those two things are really important! Your parents, other family members, doctor, and others can be part of the team that helps you reach a healthy weight. And don't go it alone when it comes to people making fun of you. Tell a parent or a teacher. Ask your friends for advice and support.

4. **Be healthy either way.** Whether someone is overweight or not, they will be healthier if they do simple things like . . .

- eat a healthy breakfast
- cut out soda
- get lots of activity

Think pink!

Jemma

And here's what other girls had to say:

Remember that you are beautiful the way you are, and it matters more on the inside anyway. When people make fun of you, look them in the eye and say, "Knock it off." If the harassing continues, alert an adult. Hope this helps!

All I can say is love that body, move that body. Work out often and eat your daily meals.

I'm overweight and I lost weight by riding my bike to school. It helps you get exercise and it helps the planet by creating less pollution!

Just get with a group of friends and stand up for yourself. That's the only way to get through the jungle called life without being eaten!

Late Bloomer Blues

Hello pink friends!

I know we've talked about this before, but I think it's worth bringing up again. Being the "late bloomer" can be hard. I know, I know, you early bloomers will say being the first one with boobs and a period, etc, is hard, too. I'm sure that's true. But today, we're going to talk about the slower-growing girls out there. If you've read the books, you know I'm one of you!

> *Dear PLS,*
>
> *Hi PLS. I love your book! I'm going into grade 7 and I still don't have my period. Quite a few of my friends already do. I feel so young. Any advice?*
>
> *Question Girl, 12*

Number one, I'd say that it's important to remember that periods happen in a wide stretch of time. Some girls are early, like ten, and other girls are later, like fifteen. It's normal, normal, normal that some girls will be later than others.

But what I think Question Girl is saying is that you still have to deal with being the less-developed one every day. I know how you feel, Question Girl. Some people might tease you about being a late bloomer. Even when they don't mean to hurt your feelings, sometimes they do. Also, no one likes feeling left out. If everyone is talking about "my period this and my period that," it's like you're not a member of their secret club.

But remember that you're part of this secret club, The Pink Locker Society (wink-wink). And also remember that you're always growing, little by little. Here's a fun activity that will prove it. Get out some photos of you over the years. Go from your cutie-pie baby stage, to preschool, to kindergarten, and on up.

Pay special attention to the last few years. Do you have a different hairstyle now? Maybe you've changed the kind of clothes you wear. And I bet you'll see that you've grown and changed quite a bit—even though you'd still like to change and grow even more.

Think pink all you late bloomers!

Jemma

And here's what other girls had to say:

Don't worry about it. I started my period only a month ago and I'm going into grade nine! Talk about late! It doesn't matter when you get your period because everyone will have one eventually! LOL

It seems really unfair that we girls have to go through all this stuff, and boys have to deal with, like, nothing.

Well, think about the big picture. If you get it now, you will have it until you are in your 50s. Talk about A LONG TIME!!

Middle School Advice Needed FAST!

Hello all you middle schoolers! If you already have a year or more of middle school under your belt, this question is for you. Our friend KGirl, 11, is starting middle school and she's pretty worried. Here's her question:

Dear PLS,

I am starting my first year of middle school and I'm sooo nervous and worried. I'm worried I'll be late to class, I won't make new friends, and I'm scared to change with everyone else in the locker room. I will have eight new teachers. What if they don't like me? PLEASE can you give me some tips and advice about middle school? Thanks!!!

KGirl, 11

Don't you just want to give KGirl a hug? I'd say it's true that middle school has new challenges: lockers, switching classes, more teachers, etc. But it's also heaps more fun than elementary school. There are so many cool things to do—new clubs, activities, sports. Even eating in the cafeteria is more fun, I think.

Any more advice for KGirl? Also, at your school this

year, please tell me you'll be nice to the sixth-graders. They need our help. Remember, even if you feel very mature now, you were once a sixth-grader, too!

Think pink!
Jemma

And here's what other girls had to say:

I felt the same way when I first started middle school. Considering I am now going into high school, I think I survived! I had four minutes between each class and surprisingly made it to each one. It doesn't seem like much, but it's a lot longer than you need. If you stop to talk to a friend on the way there, make it short. By the end of the year, I promise you will have all of this figured out.

I'm starting middle school this year too. Instead of being nervous, I decided to be excited! I can't wait! I know all these middle school things will be new, but I don't think about that part. Just chill. Relax! My plan is to make a great first impression. And, to get a "buddy" to help me through everything. Like, where to go and what to do. One of your "already" friends, who you can depend on.

Be sure to get a schedule and a school map so you can familiarize yourself with the school and teachers before the first day. There are students coming from lots of different schools. Just think how many people you will meet! ;)

Get healthy, girls!
Learn more about exercise and eating right

In *The Forever Crush,* Kate feels terrible when she learns that some of her classmates think she's fat.

No matter what you weigh, everyone can get healthier by eating more nutritious foods and being active for at least an hour each day. Try these Web sites for tips, ideas, and encouragement!

Learn to cook and you'll eat healthier. No artificial flavors. No Blue #17. Just 100 percent delicious. Even better if you can grow some of your own food. These resources can help you get started with recipes, cooking skills, and garden basics:

www.chopchopmag.com
www.spatulatta.com
www.edibleschoolyard.org

Dive into nutrition at MyPyramid.gov. You can unravel the mysteries of the U.S. Food Guide Pyramid and get solid advice about what to eat.

http://www.mypyramid.gov/kids

Discover the secrets of head-to-toe health at BAM (Body and Mind), a Web site from the U.S. Centers for Disease Control and Prevention.

www.bam.gov

Want to become a runner like Jemma? We think you can do it! Join Girls on the Run and they'll help you train for your first real race.

www.girlsontherun.org

Viva La Pink Locker Society!

Book 1

Book 2

Book 3

Book 4

Visit **www.PinkLockerSociety.org** to read excerpts, play games, and ask your own questions of Jemma and the rest of the PLS!

Tarquin Cardona

About the Author

Debra Moffitt lives in a house full of boys—with three sons and one husband. She was a newspaper reporter for more than ten years and is now the kids' editor of KidsHealth .org. That means she gets paid to write about stuff kids care about, like pimples, crushes, and puberty. She'd like to thank all the girls who visit www.pinklockersociety.org. You've asked 30,000 questions about growing up and have given tons of kind, thoughtful advice to one another. That's thinking pink!